Savage - Manhunter

Helen Dexter wanted to know who killed her husband, Harold, and Pinkerton's gave Savage the job. In Calamity, neither Sheriff Ballinger nor his deputy were that interested as they had a gang of robbers to deal with. But then there is a second widow, Mary-Lou, who has a map, possibly of a valuable mine. Now Savage must tangle with the Bloody Hills gang, led by Blackie. As a prisoner of the gang, Savage faces Poison Palmer, a killer who is not quite sane.

It isn't long before a lynch party is on the cards and in a surprise shoot-out all the mysteries are resolved.

Savage - Manhunter

SYDNEY J. BOUNDS

A Black Horse Western

ROBERT HALE · LONDON

ISBN 0 7090 7545 6

Robert Hale Limited
Clerkenwell House
Clerkenwell Green
London EC1R 0HT

Typeset by
Derek Doyle & Associates, Liverpool.
Printed and bound in Great Britain by
Antony Rowe Limited, Wiltshire

CONTENTS

CHAPTER 1

POISONED HONEYMOON

She was the only woman in the coach and probably the youngest passenger too. She gave a sigh of contentment and snuggled closer to her newly acquired husband.

'George,' she murmured, 'I'm so happy.'

George was a solid man, dressed in his new suit with a stiffened collar, fiftyish. Not the oldest there, but far from the youngest in the coach rushing them westward. Certainly the sweetest-smelling; some of the sun-baked young men – cowboys? – were trying not to stare at her. They looked uncomfortable and smelled of horses and dust and a general lack of soap and water.

It was a thrilling ride, faster than any horse could draw a carriage. *Clackety-clack, clackety-clack* sang the wheels passing over the gaps between the iron rails; beyond the window, high grass was almost yellow in the sunlight, the distant hills tinted a rich purple.

She gave another contented sigh. George was experienced in the ways of the West, a travelling man, and their future looked bright.

A small man came through the doorway connecting with the next coach, a revolver in his hand. He was followed by a heavyweight carrying an open sack, and a third man also carrying a revolver. All three had their faces covered; the first two by neckerchiefs pulled up almost to their eyes. The last man wore a black silk mask with eye-holes cut in it.

She sat upright, excited and scared; this was the Wild West.

'Keep your seats,' said the man wearing the mask. 'And your hands where we can see them. This is a hold-up. Just drop your wallets and valuables in the sack.' He spoke with an Eastern twang.

They moved along the aisle between seats, the big man holding the neck of the canvas sack open to receive contributions.

She felt George tense beside her and sensed he was about to go for the hide-out gun she knew he carried. 'No,' she whispered. 'You don't have to prove you're a hero.'

Her words came too late. The small man reached them and George lost his temper. 'You little runt, I'll—'

The small man didn't wait to find out what George had in mind. He pulled the trigger of his gun as George came out of his seat.

She heard a sharp *crack* and smelt powder burning. George fell back into his seat, staring stupidly at a red stain spreading across the front of his shirt.

The small man gave a high-pitched giggle. 'Guess that's why they call me "Poison", 'cause I give folk a dose of lead poisoning!' His voice was shrill and unnerving.

The heavyweight rumbled, 'Cut it out. The chief said not to kill passengers.'

'That's if they behave themselves. This one was going for a derringer.'

The man in the silk mask showed impatience. 'It's done now, so move along. Fill the sack and get on to the next coach.'

She stared at George and bit her lip, determined not to cry.

'Your purse,' Poison demanded. 'And rings, they must be worth something.' His eyes stared into hers and she shivered.

As he thrust his hand inside George's coat and pulled out a wallet, she eased off her rings and dropped them in the sack.

It felt like a nightmare. She could not accept that she had been married and widowed in twenty-four hours. Not even in her dreams had the West ever been this wild.

The robbers passed along the length of the coach and disappeared through the connecting doorway. In the silence someone began cursing. The train moved along as if nothing had happened.

Finally, one of the young men gathered enough courage to speak to her. He took off his hat first. 'Sure would like to help you, ma'am.'

Reality suddenly overwhelmed her; she realized her face was damp and that she was still travelling West, with no money and no one to protect her.

When Caesar lengthened his stride, Savage looked about with sharpened interest. He saw only the same low hills and barren scrub; the view seemed much the same as it had for the past several hours. Desolate, bleak and empty, now that most of the working mines had played out. Evidently Caesar disagreed.

Savage tugged the rim of his hat lower and squinted; through the dazzle of sunlight and shimmering air he detected a smudge on the horizon.

'Guess that must be Calamity,' he murmured. 'And you can smell stable hay.'

Caesar was a horse who liked to run; even after a day's steady lope, the big chestnut had legs he wanted to stretch.

I'm going soft, Savage thought, getting fond of a horse: I should have left him with Teresa.* He felt disgusted with himself, yet it gave him a warm feeling to know he was no longer a complete loner.

* See *Border Savage*, Robert Hale 2004.

The miles fled under flashing hoofs until the distant smudge grew into the town of Calamity. He passed a few shanties and then he was riding the length of Main Street; plankwalks raised above the level of the dust, a row of saloons, some boarded up, two stores, one with the hopeful sign: HODGE – *Everything for a Miner.*

Beyond a hotel, a print shop and the sheriff's office was a shingle advertising: *Doctor here.* Caesar didn't stop, or even slow, till he reached a livery stable and turned in.

Savage dismounted and stretched his legs, removed the saddle. A lethargic stableman asked, 'The usual?'

Savage frowned. 'Rub him down and feed him a mixture of oats and hay. This one's a champion.'

'That'll cost extra.'

'I hear you.'

Savage picked up his saddle-bags and shotgun and clumped along the plankwalk. He went into the first eating-place he came to – the Golden Café – and sat where he could watch the street.

'Coffee,' he told the counterman. 'A quart will do to start.' He studied a menu chalked up behind the counter: *Hash and beans – one dollar.* 'And I'll take some of that.'

The counterman, whom Savage saw had a false leg, brought a large mug filled with black coffee.

'I was one of the lucky few,' the man said. 'Not many soldiers got a leg shot off and lived.'

Savage nodded and drained the mug. 'Same again.'

He was wiping his plate clean with a chunk of bread when a man wearing a star walked through the doorway and stood studying him. A young man, with a fringe of beard and a revolver in a holster at his hip, his gaze held the penetrating assessment that policemen everywhere try to cultivate.

'Yancey,' he announced. 'Deputy sheriff. You're a stranger in town.'

'Savage. I was intending to visit your office as soon as I've eased my throat. Reckon you don't get many visitors.'

'Sheriff Ballinger's out of town, chasing train robbers. A man was shot dead.'

Savage brought a folded sheet of paper from his pocket and offered it. Yancey unfolded it, glanced at the printed heading and read: *To whom it may concern. . . .*

'A Pinkerton.' Yancey handed the paper back. 'Are you after the train robbers?'

Savage shook his head. 'Your sheriff wrote to a widow back East – name of Dexter – telling how her husband's body was found.'

The counterman poured coffee for the deputy. 'Not killed by one of us, that's for sure. We need all the business we can get!'

Yancey relaxed and sat down. 'I remember. A stranger no one knew anything about, buried and forgotten.'

'Not by his widow,' Savage said.

Yancey shrugged dismissively. 'We figured he

12

was just another body looking for a lost mine – our main business in this part of the country. I don't see what you can do.'

Savage got the impression Yancey had no further interest. 'Guess I'll nose around a little. The widow is paying Pinkerton's, and they pay me.'

'Why not? Thanks for the coffee, Timber.' The deputy hoisted himself to his feet and walked out.

Timber said, 'The fella you want to see is Hodge—'

'Why Hodge? Why not me?' The newcomer who bustled in had a red face and a pot belly. 'Everyone knows Hodge is crooked as a sidewinder. He'll tell any lie to grab your money.'

'You suggesting you don't print lies in your paper?'

Timber poured another coffee. 'This here's Wally Kemp and he owns the *Chronicle*.'

'So I have to fill pages.' Kemp reached for the mug with ink-stained fingers. 'What can I do for you, stranger? Any news of the outside world gratefully received. Where are you from? D'you know anybody in town? Staying long? On business? Confide in me and get your name in the *Chronicle*, maybe your picture too.'

His speech came out in a rush. Savage took a sip of coffee and waited.

Timber winked. 'Our Wally's always hoping for a big story. Wally, this one's a Pinkerton, so you'll need to be a mite careful what lies you tell. Remember he's got a big outfit behind him. And he says he ain't after the Bloody Hills gang.'

Kemp set down his mug and produced pencil and notebook. 'That so, stranger? You tell me what you want me to print, and that'll go in the next issue.'

'I'm looking into a death. Fella named Dexter got himself shot. D'you remember?'

'Sure I remember,' Kemp said. 'When the sheriff got word a body had been found, I rode up into the hills with him. Sheriff searched the body and found papers to identify him – by then he was beginning to smell, and small animals had been at him.

'There was no point in moving him so we dug a shallow trench – hard ground up there, you understand – and piled rocks on top. There was no clue to who killed him, or why.'

'That's something his widow will want to know.'

'Waal, keep me posted if you find anything. Maybe, after all, you'd best have a word with Hodge. He does, in his way, help to keep this town going.'

'What way's that?'

Kemp laughed. 'Why, he's our local expert on lost mines.'

'I suppose he'll be dropping in for a coffee now I've arrived?'

'No sir, not Hodge. With Hodge, you go to him.'

Savage stood up. 'Maybe I will.' He left his his saddle-bags and picked up his shotgun. 'I'll be back, Timber.'

14

'Sure thing.'

He followed the plankwalk to the store that boasted *Everything for a Miner.* and it looked as if it might. Outside were racks of picks and shovels, lamps and coils of rope and some tools Savage didn't recognize; inside he found denim overalls, heavy boots and helmets and canvas haversacks. Behind a long counter were shelves and pigeon-holes filled with documents.

Hodge sat in a revolving chair, a lanky man with long skinny arms and legs, a spider at the centre of his web. He wore a derby hat and was smoking a cigar.

As Savage approachad, he removed the cigar from his lips to chant, 'I can show you maps and charts, I can show you mines and sell you shares. Lost mines, secret mines, hidden mines are my business. I have the finest selection in the West and I'm the only honest dealer. Trust Hodge.'

Savage was impressed, but ignored the last bit. New York had been full of Hodges, known to the police as confidence men.

'I also hire out burros—'

'It's information I'm after.'

'—and sell information.'

Savage smiled. 'I don't get unlimited expenses for buying information.'

'Then you'll need to take lessons with me – for a suitable fee – in adjusting your expenses.'

'Do you remember Harold Dexter?'

'There's nothing wrong with my memory. Did

15

anyone tell you I was the one who found him?'

'No one did,' Savage acknowledged. 'Did you recognize him?'

Hodge shook his head decisively. 'He wasn't anyone I'd dealt with. Never seen him before.'

After a pause, he asked, 'Who are you working for?'

'His widow hired Pinkerton's.'

Hodge studied him carefully. 'You're staying at the hotel?'

Savage nodded.

'Tomorrow morning, early, I'll saddle a couple of burros and take you into the hills. I'll show you exactly where I found him.'

'Fine.'

Savage left, picked up his saddle-bags at Timber's Golden Café and booked a room at Calamity's one and only hotel.

CHAPTER 2

VALLEY OF
LAWLESS MEN

After breakfast Savage walked to the livery stable to make sure Caesar was being properly looked after. The stallion's ugly head nuzzled his shirt pocket until Savage gave him the sugar lumps he'd put there.

'You might have him well trained,' the stable-man said, 'but that one's got the devil in him.'

'Treat him right and you've nothing to fear.'

Savage stroked the chestnut and murmured, 'Not today, Caesar. You get good and rested for tomorrow, who knows?'

Satisfied his horse was cared for, Savage carried his shotgun along to Hodge's place. Two burros waited patiently in the dusty street, and Hodge stepped outside, slapping a derby on his head.

17

'Have you ridden one of these before?'

'I've been on a mule recently.'

Hodge nodded. 'Good enough. Leave yours be and he'll follow my mare.'

He gave his animal a kick-start and they went forward, out of town towards the hills. It was a long, slow climb and Savage watched the land. The trail wound upwards, the ground uneven with only a few patches of short grass.

Hodge paused once at a spring to let the burros drink and Savage asked, 'How come you found the body?'

'I take a regular trip around the claims I hold. One day, some prospector's going to make a strike and Calamity won't be just a town hanging on from one failed mine to the next. And I'll take my cut.'

Higher up was a bare and arid land composed of boulders and jagged rocks with a few thorn bushes. Hodge dismounted when they came to a section of wooden planking nailed across an opening in the hillside.

'Entrance to an old mine. This is where I found him.'

Savage looked around and saw nothing out of place. 'Why should someone from the East fall for a lost mine story?'

Hodge pushed his hat to the back of his head to reveal a few strands of almost white hair. He lit a cigar and inhaled. 'Waal now, folk who reckon they're a mite superior usually fall easiest of all. A

18

mark can rarely resist a chance of something for nothing.'

He pointed to a small pile of rocks a little way off. 'That wasn't there before, so it'll be where the sheriff buried him.'

'I suppose you didn't hesitate to help yourself to anything on the body?'

Hodge drew on his cigar till the end glowed. 'You have a suspicious mind, but why should the killer leave anything of value?'

'Maybe his idea of value is different from yours.'

'Maybe. I looked, but there was nothing useful enough for me to risk getting in bad with the sheriff.' /

'Was he a miner?'

'Not a prospector, if that's what you mean, but we see a lot of Easterners looking to get rich quick. They don't last long.'

Savage scouted the area and Hodge watched with an air of disbelief. 'Think you'll learn anything after this time?'

'I'm paid to look, so I look. Who knows what might show up.'

What showed up, after they made a meal and set off down the hillside was the sheriff's posse, a weary bunch of men returning from a chase.

Sheriff Ballinger was middle-aged, overweight and unhappy. He mopped sweat from his face as they joined him.

'This fella's a Pinkerton,' Hodge said.

Ballinger gave a grunt. 'So? Does he figure to

19

grab the reward on that gang in the Bloody Hills when I can't even find them? Is that what you're telling me?'

'Nope. Says he's looking into the Dexter shooting.'

'Dexter?' The sheriff seemed at a loss and it took a couple of minutes for the name to register. 'Oh, him. Who cares?'

'Apparently his widow does,' Savage said mildly, 'so I'd appreciate any help you give me, Sheriff.'

'Are you joking? He was shot by a person unknown. We identified the corpse and notified next of kin. That's it.'

Ballinger, Savage realized, was a political appointment, and no man-hunter. He went through the motions to appear good and his posse was only interested in reaching a saloon to drink their fee.

Savage rode alongside Hodge on the way back to Calamity and their burros had no difficulty keeping up with the tired horses.

'You, Hodge,' Ballinger growled. 'Have you been making up stories again?'

'Just showing the man where the body lies. Live and let live, Sheriff. You and this Pinkerton are paid. Me – and those you're hunting – have to get a living any way we can. Railroads, banks make sure they grab their profit first.'

'Don't talk to me about banks and railroads – or ranchers and stage operators. All I get,' the sheriff complained, 'are moans and groans. Get our money back! Stop this gang – some hope!'

He rode on in a depressed silence.

'Poison' Palmer sat apart from the rest of the gang. The walls of the valley were high, the canyon entrance not obvious; even so Blackie insisted on a guard, night and day. Palmer didn't much like the man who wore the black silk mask, but he had to admit their leader used his brain.

They could all relax because the wood cabins and camp-fire were not overlooked. The evening meal finished, the train robbers sat smoking and passing a bottle, telling tales and laughing.

All kinds of drifters gathered in the valley: out-of-work cowboys who'd rounded up a few head of cattle; casual thieves; gunmen wanted by the law; horse rustlers – a pool of talent from which Blackie could pick and choose as he needed.

Palmer didn't fit in; he didn't drink and he didn't smoke, and he had his own kind of amusement. Blackie didn't approve, but Palmer had a talent; he could frighten people, and a scared man was more likely to run than fight.

Nothing worried him; he was a loner and tended to avoid normal human contact.

The sun had almost disappeared and shadows were darker and lengthening; soon there would only be starlight to see by. Palmer liked to kill; he enjoyed taking life, and inflicting pain was his idea of entertainment.

He'd snared a prairie dog for this evening's

amusement and now casually broke both back legs before he released it, so it couldn't get too far from him.

He watched it crawl, whimpering, scared, and a warm feeling spread through his body. Saliva fell from his lips and his eyes sparkled. It was not the same as having a man to torment – or, better still, a woman – but better than nothing.

He admired some of the Indian tribes, those who had brought torture to a peak of agony; he could only hope to achieve similar results after long practice.

Blackie disapproved – soft, Palmer sneered – and he was backed by Big Jake, but most of the gang didn't care one way or the other. And Palmer had his excuse ready . . . 'Boys always torture small animals, don't they? I've never really grown up . . . I'm just a boy at heart.'

He unsheathed a long slender blade, one he'd spent hours honing to a razor edge. He held the prairie dog firmly, feeling it squirm under his hand. He brought the shining blade close to the animal. Frightened eyes stared up, hypnotized. It squealed.

Smiling, Palmer brought the point of the blade down, slowly, to slit open the tiny belly. Gently, almost reverently, he pulled out its insides and held them up before the animal's eyes.

It knew pain, he could read that; it knew fear. It was dying, without hope of deliverance, and began to shake in his hand.

He watched till the eyes glazed over, getting intense pleasure from its last exhalation of breath. As the small body stiffened in death he threw it away.

When the posse rode into Calamity, Hodge and Savage peeled off. Hodge took both burros to stabling behind his store and Savage walked to the hotel. There seemed no point in trying to talk to the sheriff until he was in a better mood.

The hotelman sat behind his desk in the hall, using a rolled-up copy of the *Chronicle* in an attempt to swat a fly. He paused to survey Savage with more than casual interest.

'I have to say, even if you are the first Pinkerton agent I've met, you don't look a ladies man to me.'

Savage slowed to a standstill. 'So?'

The hotelman jerked a skinny thumb at the staircase. 'The room at the top, turn left, first door. Only the best will do for her ladyship. Wants to see you, pronto, soon as you show, meaning now.'

'Did the lady give a name?'

'Not to me. You expecting more than one?'

'I wasn't expecting anybody.'

The hotelman looked disappointed and pursued the fly annoying him.

Savage moved quietly up the stairs. At the top, he levelled his shotgun to cover the room and kicked open the door.

A woman sat on the edge of the bed, facing an open window. She turned her head as the door crashed back against the wall and calmly appraised him.

Savage saw there was no one else in the room and lowered his gun.

'Are you the Pinkerton agent? I'm Helen Dexter. In future you will knock on the door and wait to be invited in. Remember that I'm paying your wages.' Her voice was educated, and icy.

'No one told me you were coming.'

'I don't have to tell anyone. What have you discovered so far?'

'Only that your husband has been buried and forgotten. Nobody wants to know.'

'I want to know,' she said firmly. 'He had a map with him, showing the route to an old mine. What happened to that?'

Savage stepped into the room and shut the door behind him. 'Maybe his killer took it.'

'That answer is not satisfactory.'

Savage watched her. Could she really be as calm as she appeared? She had a slender build, short dark hair and wore expensive and fashionable clothes.

'Someone killed Harry and the law has failed him. He's entitled to justice, like anyone else, and I'm here to see he gets it. Is the sheriff back yet?'

'He's back,' Savage confirmed, 'but I suggest you leave him till morning. By then he may be in a more helpful mood.'

She hesitated. 'Very well. I don't like it, but I'll accept your advice.'

Savage let his gaze rove over her, the way a man does when considering a woman's potential in bed.

'No,' she said flatly. 'I'm not available to you. You remind me too much of Harry – the same restlessness, always ready to move on.'

Savage could understand that; he would be too, married to this one.

'I tried to make something of him,' she said, 'and I thought things were going well – until someone sent him an old map of a mine.'

'Who?'

'I have no idea. Harry left in a rush, promising to send for me when he'd made his fortune.'

Savage repressed a laugh; hundreds of married men must have used that excuse in recent years.

Helen Dexter said, 'Now that I'm here, I shall take charge of this investigation.'

CHAPTER 3

DEATH OF A HORSE

The sheriff's office was crowded. Ballinger slumped behind his desk with Helen Dexter facing him; she sat stiffly upright in a wooden chair as if not even morning sunlight could melt her icy disposition.

'I want an accounting of what you've done, Mr Ballinger,' she said calmly. 'And of what you've found out, and I would like that first.'

Deputy Yancey and Savage leaned against opposite walls, fascinated; only the faintest ghost of a smile on each of their faces betrayed their amusement.

A prisoner in the cell at the rear of the office lent his support. 'That's right, lady, tell him his fortune. All he's good for is locking up a fella who's taken a drink too many. If that's possible.'

Savage thought he might be tempted to take to

drink before long. He resented the way she was trying to take over his investigation. He'd warned her off, pointing out that she was not familiar with the ways of Western men, but she seemed deaf to common sense.

She had smiled in a condescending manner. 'Oh, I'll leave all the manly bits to you. I'll simply direct your efforts from here.'

Ballinger turned his head to glare into the cell.

'Another peep out of you, Mac, and I'll have a word with every saloonkeeper in town. You'll never be served another drink while I'm sheriff.'

He turned back and forced a smile. 'Mrs Dexter, try to be reasonable. Things are handled differently here from back East. I identified the body and notified your own authorities; then we buried him. The heat spoils a body quickly and, in the wilderness, scavengers close in pretty damn soon.'

'And his murderer? He was shot, I understand.'

'Yes, he was shot at close range and, apparently, unarmed. But you need to remember the local law officers – me and my deputy – cover a big area and sometimes one job has to wait on another. Right now I have important people breathing down my neck and demanding I get rid of a whole gang of robbers and outlaws plaguing this county. You have no idea how—'

She cut in sharply, 'I have an idea you've done little to find my husband's murderer.'

'If he was one of this gang – Blackie's gang – he's likely hiding out somewhere in the Bloody Hills.'

'Harry carried a map showing an old mine. I understand that is missing.'

'There was nothing like that on him. That I can be sure of.'

Deputy Yancey drawled, 'It occurs to me that it doesn't have to be Blackie's gang at all. Remember, Hodge claims he was first to find the body – and he deals in maps.'

Ballinger's face flushed. 'If I thought that, I'd shut him down.'

Mac's sardonic laugh came from the cell at the back. 'Stop dreaming. Hodge is way ahead of you every time.'

Helen Dexter rose abruptly, smoothing down her skirt. 'Mr Savage, I suggest you investigate this gang the sheriff talks about. Attempt to decide if one or more of its members were responsible. I shall speak to Mr Hodge myself.'

As she swept from the office, Yancey whistled. 'Just like that, "attempt to decide if—"'

Even Sheriff Ballinger managed a faint smile. 'Head for the Bloody Hills, Mr Savage, and you'll be going in the right direction. But I can't tell you how to penetrate that barrier.'

Yancey added, 'And good luck!'

Savage walked outside and took the opposite direction to Helen Dexter. At the livery, he saddled Caesar and rode out of town. He just rode at first, pleased to be free of Pinkerton's client. Then, remembering the direction the posse had come from, he turned his horse and headed that way.

The trail climbed to where a few gaunt trees struggled to survive, levelled off for a few miles and began to descend. Where a stream trickled down from the hills he paused to fill his water bottle and then let Caesar set their pace.

The stallion began to run, but not for long; the sun had baked the ground brick hard and grass gave way to scrub and cacti. This land was hardly more than a stony desert, arid; the gentlest breeze lifted dust so Savage hoisted his neckerchief to mask his mouth and nostrils.

Eventually he glimpsed his destination; a wall of red sandstone rising to the sky; as a barrier to travel, the Bloody Hills were well named.

He approached slowly. The rock face was steep, almost vertical, and he angled across it to observe each shadowed crevice. Somewhere along its length one of those crevices must open into a passageway through the wall. He rode on until a shrill voice challenged, 'Where d'yuh think you're going, fella?'

Savage reined back, eyes searching the red rock. Sunlight reflected from the barrel of a rifle and he caught a glimpse of a small man covering him from shifting shadow.

He pulled his neckerchief down and wiped dust from his face.

'I'm looking for sanctuary,' he called. 'I heard this was a safe place to hide from the law.'

The small man gave a cackle of laughter that made Savage's skin crawl. 'Sure is – for us!'

Caesar lowered his head; he'd discovered a few

29

tufts of grass to nibble and, step by step, drifted closer to the cleft in the rock face.

'That'll do,' the small man said. 'Stand still just where you are.'

Savage knew he'd made a mistake when he felt the hairs lift at the back of his scalp. The small man jerked his trigger finger and Caesar shuddered and sank slowly to the dirt.

'Now start walking, Pinkerton!' The last word came out loaded with venom.

Savage rolled clear of the still quivering animal. That anyone should shoot a horse to get the man was worse than murder. He lost his self-control, lifted his shotgun and fired off both barrels; the range was too great to be effective and the rifleman laughed.

Savage reverted to what he had always been; a wild man. He shook with rage and his lip curled back in an animal snarl. He rammed in two more shells, and might have hurled himself across the distance between them, but the small man gave another of his nerve-freezing cackles.

Savage's hat sailed away as a further shot came. For a moment his gaze locked with mad staring eyes and then the sun, hammering on his bare head, broke his frenzy and brought him back to reality. He realized he was no more than target practice for the hidden marksman.

He dropped down behind the body of his horse; at least now he could stop the rifleman approaching to finish him off. He clamped a lid on the violence still building inside him; the small man had shot his partner and he would pay for that. This investigation had become personal.

Cooling, he admitted he'd gone soft over a horse, but now the savage in him was back in charge. He could wait; first he had to survive, then he would return.

'Cooled your ardour, wild boy?' the small man jeered, and aimed and triggered again. This time he punctured Savage's water bottle, hanging from his saddle; and Savage watched the precious liquid drain away.

He decided he must withdraw, and wormed his body across the barren soil, keeping the carcass of his horse between him and the rifleman. He reached a group of small rocks and wriggled between them for cover and shade.

The rifleman winged a shot overhead; it screeched as it ricocheted away. Savage didn't think the man would venture nearer, knowing he had a shotgun, and settled to wait.

He watched the sun and the lengthening shadows and waited. He heard his tormentor call, 'You thirsty, boy? I've got water here – why don't yuh come and get it?'

Savage ignored the taunting voice; he endured the remaining hours of daylight and then started to walk back the way he had come. The killer of Caesar had a short reprieve.

He walked steadily across the parched and bone-hard land towards Calamity.

*

Hodge watched her move along the plankwalk with a calculating eye. She took short, quick steps. Even a small town housed a few women, but a smartly dressed Easterner was a rare sight.

He crushed out the butt of a cigar and straightened the derby on his head; he thought he'd passed the age when he allowed a woman to interfere with business, but. . . .

She paused in the doorway, looking around; probably she only noticed the dust. Then her gaze settled on him and she advanced. Her smile was cold.

'You are Mr Hodge?'

'Yep.' He decided, almost without thinking, to be a laconic Westerner.

'And you found my husband's body?'

'Yep.'

'Did you find a map on him?'

She paused, not sure what to ask next, and Hodge thought he'd better help her out. 'A map of a mine, was it?'

'Yes indeed, and Harry was wonderfully excited—'

'Mine have a name?'

'I didn't notice. At that time I wasn't interested. The sheriff hinted—'

'I can guess. Take a look at this.' He reached behind him, selected a map from a pigeon-hole and spread it out on the counter. 'Recognize it?'

She looked surprised. 'Is this—'

'Nope. This is the mine nearest to where I found him.'

Her face registered doubt and he showed her others; she recognized none. Hodge was patient. Obviously she had seen a map, but he no longer believed she would know it again.

'Maybe the map had nothing to do with his death?' he suggested.

'Then why should he have been killed?'

'Men kill for all sorts of reasons – or no reason at all.'

'I can't believe that.'

Meaning, Hodge thought, she didn't want to believe it.

'It was the map, I'm sure.' Her voice was no longer calm. 'This mine must be worth a great deal, and it belongs to me!'

Hooked, thought Hodge with satisfaction. Property was what Mrs Dexter was all about. Likely she had considered her husband property, and that was why he'd run. Savage was her agent and she regarded him, too, as property. For the first time since she'd entered his shop, he cracked a smile.

That was not how he read the Pinkerton.

The stars guided him, or he might have been in serious trouble. A long walk stretched before him and he needed to conserve energy. After the heat of day, he settled into a steady stride.

The desert sky reached to every horizon and towered higher than he could visualize, darker than the deepest mine. He walked beneath an ocean of stars, more than he'd dreamed existed, each bright and clear as a gemstone. It was so different from New York at night. He realized he'd never seen the sky before, only a small part of it through a haze of smoke, with starlight dimmed to a faint twinkle. He was even a little awed.

The temperature dropped just as steadily; one foot in front of the other and his gaze on the constellations.

He took a short break after what he judged to be an hour; he sat on a flat rock and removed each boot in turn to shake the dust out.

Dust got everywhere; his eyes, ears, nostrils; when he cleared his throat he spat out dust. The slightest breeze lifted the surface of the land. If he stumbled over a half-buried rock with one step, with the next he sank inches deep.

He paused beside a cactus taller than most, sliced into it with his Bowie and squeezed out a few drops of moisture. Refreshed, he went on again.

Another hour passed and he transferred his gaze to the distant hills where, he knew, a stream trickled cool, clear water. In his mind he could see it, scoop it up with cupped hands and taste it.

The temperature kept falling and he began to shiver. During the next hour his leg muscles protested about the strain he was putting on them. His eyes had a tendency to close and he walked blindly, knowing he must reach water before the sun rose again.

It was a punishing journey, the ground uneven; there were moments when he stumbled, weary of the unending desert. He was tempted to sink to the ground and sleep, but resisted the urge. The intense cold helped, setting his teeth chattering.

He remembered the rifleman calling him 'Pinkerton'; the man had known in advance to expect him, and that meant the gang had a spy in Calamity.

He thought of Caesar, casually shot to set him afoot, and anger kept him going.

He imagined Teresa, the young Mexican who'd won a race on Caesar's back. He wouldn't want to face her until he'd tracked down the horse killer and put an end to him.

He was staggering when the sun crept above the horizon.

CHAPTER 4

THE SECOND
MRS DEXTER

Wally Kemp had a job to keep still. He wanted action and he was just sitting with a mug of cooling coffee in Timber's Golden Café. It often seemed to him that he spent most of his life waiting for a news story to break.

He'd set type to announce the arrival of a Pinkerton detective, and Dexter's widow, and the failure of the sheriff's posse to catch the railroad robbers. Now he waited for the stagecoach to arrive. It ran most days, but didn't always call at Calamity; the town was on a loop off the main trail and the stage called only if passengers were booked for it.

'What d'yuh make of the Pinkerton, Timber?'

'Reckon it's a shame he ain't after this gang. I'd

put my money on him to find 'em before Ballinger, or Yancey.'

Kemp nodded. 'Yancey ain't as popular as he likes to think. Especially with older men.'

'He's young yet. Reckon Sheriff'll lick him into shape.'

'Hodge is keeping quiet—'

The elderly counterman snorted. 'Hodge doesn't have anything to sell, yet.'

They heard the creaking of the coach and saw dust rising before the driver yelled and braked outside the hotel opposite.

'This here's Calamity. All out who's getting out!'

Kemp came to his feet, reaching in his pocket for a notebook and pencil as he crossed the road.

Two passengers descended from the coach, a man with a carpet bag, and a woman waiting for the driver to offload her trunk.

'I represent the *Chronicle*.' Kemp spoke his set piece. 'News of the outside world always welcome. If you're thinking of staying, subscribers are even more welcome.'

The man with the carpet bag turned on a professional smile; he was thin and wore a suit with a watch and chain. He had sideburns and a slim moustache and when he spoke a single gold tooth flashed.

'Tell your readers Johnny Nelson's in town. I'm a sporting gent – cards, dice or whatever's your fancy – I'll cover any bet on anything at any time. You name it.'

Kemp turned to the woman. 'And you, ma'am?' He was being polite; anyone could see she was a saloon woman, an artificial blonde, her face hidden beneath powder and paint.

'Mary-Lou,' she offered.

'This lady,' Nelson said, 'is under my protection. She is a widowed lady and has recently come into possession of a valuable mine.'

He paused, briefly, and a small derringer appeared in his hand, and vanished. 'I'm here to see she's not cheated of her inheritance.'

Kemp managed to keep a smile from his face. 'What mine is that?'

'We're keeping the name to ourselves for the present.'

'That's wise!'

Mary-Lou said, 'Luckily I have a copy of his map, so when I read in the paper that my husband was dead, I decided to see for myself if this mine is worth anything.'

'And your husband's name?'

'Harold Dexter.'

Wally Kemp's enthusiasm came to a boil. He barely restrained a shout of joy. Now he had a story: one dead man and two widows, both after the same mine and staying in the same hotel.

Savage limped into Calamity in a bad mood. He'd refreshed his body at a stream, but he needed food and sleep before anything else. And his priorities had changed.

Identifying Dexter's murderer had been pushed to the back of his brain; his forebrain was filled by a need to lay hands on the bastard who had shot Caesar.

He paused at the sheriff's office and slid into a chair.

Ballinger was seated at his desk, contemplating paperwork with a glum expression. He glanced up, then stared. 'What happened to you?'

'I found one of your gang and he shot my horse under me. If you locate the carcass, you'll be close to an entrance to the valley.'

Ballenger made a faint smile. 'Maybe, but that doesn't mean I'll find a posse willing to ride into a trap.'

'Another point,' Savage said. 'You've got someone in town feeding them information. He knew I was a Pinkerton.'

'That doesn't surprise me. More than once I've had a suspicion they anticipated where my posse would ride.'

'So, now I need some information – you probably have a few ideas about this gang. The one I met was small and had some kind of a weird laugh. Killing came easy to him. A rifleman. Do you have a name?'

Ballinger opened a drawer in his desk and brought out a batch of Wanted notices; he flipped through them, selected one and passed it across. 'Recognize him?'

Savage saw a narrow face with a feral look about it, eyes that seemed to have a fixed stare. He checked the description for height: *five feet, four inches.* That was about right.

Abel Palmer, he read, *called 'Poison' Palmer. Known to kill at the slightest provocation. Wanted for murder in three states.*

'This fits what I could see of him.'

Ballinger grimaced. 'It's only right to warn you – he has a reputation as mad, bad, and dangerous.'

Savage handed back the notice without comment. 'Thanks.' He walked outside and along to the Golden Café.

Timber poured coffee into a large mug and stumped around the end of the counter to place it before him.

'You look rough, so get that down yuh. Hash coming up pronto. Have you seen the second widow yet?'

'Right now I'm interested in two things only. Food, then sleep.'

'Wally met her off the stage. She claims to be Dexter's wife too.'

Savage merely grunted.

'Her name's Mary-Lou and she looks experienced. She has a gambler in tow – for protection, he says. Seems she has a map.'

Savage's interest sharpened. 'That might be worth a look.'

Timber brought him a platter filled with hash, a plate of beans, and bread. Savage ate like a man with an empty stomach while the counterman rambled on.

'Wally's over at the hotel, waiting. I guess most of Calamity's waiting to see what happens when they meet. I mean, two widows of the same husband in the same hotel could get real lively.'

Savage cleaned both plates, drained another mug of coffee and found his eyes had a tendency to close. He paid Timber and crossed the street.

In the hotel lobby, Wally Kemp was like a pan of water on the boil, bubbling with excitement. 'They haven't met yet, but I think—'

'Not now,' Savage brushed past the newspaper-man and went up the stairs.

The door of Helen Dexter's room was ajar, and she hissed, 'Where have you been? I was told—'

Savage didn't pause. 'Later.'

He went into his room, kicked the door shut and propped a chair under the doorknob. He pulled off his boots and lay flat on his back on the bed. In seconds he was fast asleep.

Something was on, Palmer felt sure of that. Blackie, carrying his telescope, had climbed the red cliffs to the look-out point half an hour before. Now he was coming down. At the bottom, he detoured to one of the cabins and spoke to Big Jake.

Palmer went on honing his blade, watching the pair of them head towards him. Jake didn't scare him; he was big and strong but slow, and Palmer knew he could have a knife in him before he lifted a hand.

They passed Virgil, a one-time cowboy, practising with his rope. 'Any action, boss?'

'Not yet.'

They stopped in front of him and Blackie didn't look happy. He was an Easterner, of course, but seemed paler than usual.

When Blackie spoke, there was a hint of anxiety in his voice. 'You failed to stop the Pinkerton. Why did you disobey orders?'

'Who says I did? I shot his horse, didn't I? D'you think he's going to walk out of that desert?'

'That's exactly what he did, Palmer. He's back in Calamity.'

Palmer shifted his gaze from Blackie to Jake, and back. 'I can't believe that ... but you know what I'm like, boss.' A whine crept into his voice and he stared at the ground. 'I can't think straight sometimes. My head hurts.'

'That's why I do your thinking for you,' Blackie said. 'That's why you need to obey me in everything, in detail, always.'

Big Jake nodded solemnly. 'A mistake, Poison.'

'Yes, this time you didn't obey me, and so there's the carcass of a horse left to mark our canyon entrance to this valley for anyone to see.'

'A live horse would have wandered away to find fresh fodder someplace else. You have to obey the chief.'

'I can't help it,' Palmer whined. 'I'm sick in the head, remember?'

'You made a serious mistake,' Blackie insisted.

'It's up to you to get rid of that tell-tale carcass. I don't care how – just do it!'

When Savage woke, daylight was fading. From the window he saw lights coming on and heard the sounds of men starting an evening's drinking.

He pulled on his boots and went downstairs and along a passage to the outhouse behind the hotel. After relieving himself, he splashed water over his face and hands at the pump in the yard.

His brain began to function again. Another widow, someone had said, with a map. But at the top of the stairs, Helen Dexter waited for him beside a half-open door. Her lips made a thin line until she spoke.

'If you are quite rested, perhaps you now have something to report?'

'Only that I got my horse shot and had a long walk back. I need to talk to this other woman.'

Helen sniffed. 'Next room,' she said, and banged her door shut.

Savage collected his shotgun before he went calling. The woman sat before a mirror, carefully painting her face. The man stood watching her, rolling a cigarette with expert fingers. Savage recognized his type straight off.

' 'Evening all,' he said. 'I represent Mrs Helen Dexter.'

The man looked mildly interested. 'A Pinkerton, is that right?'

Savage nodded, and the woman said, 'Harry left

her, you know. He married me after that.'

The man added quickly, 'So anything Dexter left belongs to Mary-Lou.'

'I've been told you have a map,' Savage said. 'I'd like to see it.'

The gambling man lost his easy smile. 'No. I sure ain't trusting you that far.' His hand moved casually towards an inside pocket.

Savage brought up his shotgun. 'I'm not looking for trouble, but you might just lose some fingers if this goes off.'

The gambler quickly put his hands behind his back, and Mary-Lou said, 'Why don't you take a walk, Johnny? Leave this to me.'

Johnny eased himself to the door and outside, closing it after him. His feet clattered going down the stairs.

Mary-Lou sat on the edge of the bed and smiled at Savage; she had long hair and a full figure. She patted the turned-down sheet beside her. 'Why don't you relax? Johnny's not the jealous sort.'

'That's lucky, but I still want to see this map of yours.'

'It's a copy I made when Harry was asleep. He prized it so maybe it's really worth something. Who knows?' She shrugged. 'But I don't have it now – Johnny won't let it out of his possession, so forget it.'

She started to undress and Savage found himself becoming excited; it was a while since he'd been with a woman.

'You might help me,' she suggested.

Savage pushed her back across the bed and tore at her dress. His grip tightened as he sprawled over her.

She struggled. 'Wait, damn you – clothes cost money!'

But he wasn't in a waiting mood. There was a fierce anger inside him, the memory of Caesar sinking to the ground in slow motion, the unexpected pain because he'd allowed himself to care.

In his need for revenge he wanted to hurt someone, anyone. He tugged at his belt and got his pants down, thrusting inside her as if she were responsible, breathless and panting. He attacked her like a barbarian looting a citadel.

'Jeez,' she murmured, clinging to him. 'You're a savage . . . but I've got to admit it beats looking at some old map!'

Palmer left his horse with the guard in the canyon and carried an axe, newly sharpened, a hammer and a large piece of sacking. His arrival disturbed a clutch of vultures feeding on the carcass of the Pinkerton's horse. They continued feeding until he raised his rifle, then flapped their wings to take off and circle overhead.

There were still great slabs of flesh attached to the bones and he swung his axe viciously, slicing into the muscles and working up a rhythm. At first he was disgusted with Blackie and Jake; personally he didn't give a damn who found the carcass or what they did afterwards. Then he began to enjoy his work and felt almost grateful to the boss. The one disappointment was the lack of blood.

He tossed chunks of meat into the air and watched the birds swoop; they were no good at catching on the wing but settled to feed where it landed.

The smell could have put some men off; not him. Palmer remembered men butchering a steer for a barbecue when he was a boy; he'd been thrilled and learnt to appreciate the smell of death. His first job had been helping in a butcher's shop, until he'd killed a man and had to run for it.

He chopped, dismembering the carcass joint by joint; it seemed a long time since he'd enjoyed himself so much. The last piece of flesh was carved away and he paused to wipe sweat from his face. Then he picked up his hammer and began to smash the bones; he found it hard work.

'I should have thought to bring a saw,' he grumbled. 'I'll forget my head one day.' He cackled with laughter. 'That's why they call a doc a sawbones, 'cause it makes the job easier!'

He went on swinging and smashing, sending out showers of splinters, until the last bone was in pieces, and he regarded his work with satisfaction. 'That's me, "Butcher" Palmer!'

He brought his horse from the canyon and spread the sacking over the ground, tying one end to his saddle; then he heaped bones on to it. He started the horse walking and swung into the saddle.

He dragged the sack of bones behind him along the bottom of the red rock wall.

Each bump in the ground dislodged a few pieces of bone, scattering them widely; scavengers followed, making his mount skittish.

'A job well done,' he said proudly. 'Blackie should be proud of me.'

And he remembered the Pinkerton who'd caused all this trouble. 'I'd like to use him the same way, he thought. Maybe I will when I get my hands on him!'

CHAPTER 5

SLEIGHT OF HAND

Sheriff Ballinger sat in his office, listening to his
deputy. Yancey was amused by the situation.

'Two women, each claiming to be his widow –
this Dexter must have had something other
husbands haven't got.'

Ballinger sighed. His deputy was young, his
beard half-grown and his star polished till it shone.

'Frank,' he warned, 'keep out of this. Never
come between two women sharing an interest in
the same man. They can be devils when they're
roused.' He changed the subject. 'Did I tell you
what the Pinkerton said?'

Yancey inclined his head.

'Waal, I've given it some thought, and I want you
to ride out there. Take a close look at the wall
where the carcass is – see if you can spot a way
through the cliffs.'

48

'You don't want me to ride into the valley. I hope?'

'No, Frank, just look around, fix any likely entrance in your mind, then come back and tell me. Folk are getting fed up with Blackie's raids and, one day, we'll muster a posse the size of an army. If we come up with a way in we'll look good.'

'Gotcha.' Yancey seemed impressed, but still reluctant to miss the fun. After a pause he said, 'There could be trouble between Nelson and this Pinkerton.'

'Nothing I can't handle, Frank.' Because he patrolled the saloons in the evening, his deputy seemed to think he was some kind of town-tamer. 'One more thing – before you ride out, put your star in your pocket. Sunlight reflecting off that can make you a target.'

Yancey's mood stayed light-hearted. He said, 'You're the boss,' and left to get his horse.

Hodge was eating his noonday meal when Savage arrived at his store. 'Smells good,' he said.

'A boy brings it from Timber each day.'

There was only one chair and Hodge was in it so Savage up-ended a bucket and sat on that. 'You don't believe in making your customers comfortable?'

'I don't want time-wasters looking for somewhere to squat while they wag their tongues. I'm a one-man business – say your piece and move along.'

'Has Johnny Nelson been here?'

'Yep.'

'Did he show you a map?'

'Nope.' Hodge forked pie into his mouth and chewed slowly. 'He asked me if I knew of a mine in the Bloody Hills.' Hodge laughed at the best joke since Calamity got its name.

Savage waited patiently.

'There's only the one as far as I know, and if that's what the fuss is about, the joke's on both widows.'

He took another mouthful of pie and used a tooth-pick to remove a piece of stringy meat.

'It was well known before Blackie and his gang moved in – and no one's going to dispute their territory – well known because it had been salted, and more than once, I suspect, to attract the innocent.'

'But that's not where you found Dexter's body.'

'Nowhere near,' Hodge agreed.

'Do you have a map of this mine? Does it have a name?'

'Oh, it has a name – the Last Hope. I no longer have a map – not even I could sell that one today.'

'But someone killed Dexter. Could he have got a copy of it?'

'That wouldn't be difficult. Maps get copied all the time and sold on. And copies of copies, not always accurate. That's all part of the business.'

Savage left him feeding his face. There was something going on he didn't understand;

50

perhaps a look at Mary-Lou's map would help. He considered ways of getting his hands on it. By the time he reached the hotel, he decided he needed to talk to Helen Dexter.

Oil lamps gave a warm and friendly glow to the interior of the Bonanza saloon as Savage pushed through the batwings. He walked between the tables to the long counter and said, 'A small beer.'

The barman nodded. 'Heard about yuh – my name's Ben Ford, and I run a quiet bar.' He lifted a stout axe-handle from beneath the counter. 'This says so.'

Savage looked at him; a pug face, thick-set body with red suspenders over a flannel shirt, sleeves rolled up to show a bruiser's muscles.

He nodded gravely. 'Quiet is the way I like it, Mr Ford.'

The barman poured and Savage stood with one foot on the brass rail, sipping warily and studying the lay-out in the mirror behind the bar.

Johnny Nelson sat in a card game, smoking a thin cigarette, and it appeared that his whole attention was on the cards in his hand. The other players were drinking steadily.

Mary-Lou circulated among the tables smiling and introducing herself. When she reached him, Savage offered, 'Buy you a drink?'

'Whiskey.' The barman poured and she tossed her drink back with a practised hand and moved on.

Savage watched Johnny Nelson's fingers, supple and deft with cards and, certainly, with other things too. A concealed derringer was more than a possibility. He studied his pockets where they bulged slightly, and the wide sleeves and hang of his coat; tailored to his requirements. After a time he felt sure where Nelson kept the map.

Savage set down his half-empty glass and moved to the doorway. He looked towards the hotel, diagonally across the street. There was a light in the window of Helen Dexter's room.

As he showed himself, the light went out. He returned to the bar to keep an eye on Nelson's game, remembering his own early days when he worked the dew York dockside. . . .

. . . the smell of fish as they were gutted and chucked into wooden tubs was strong; gulls screamed as they dive-bombed to snatch any scrap. The waterway was noisy with tugs and paddle-steamers; further along, a tall-masted schooner swung gently at anchor.

Passengers streamed ashore, looking for porters or cabs. Freight was unloaded and stacked, or reloaded onto horse-drawn wagons; trunks and travelling bags were piled high on the docking pier, waiting for owners to claim them. Friends and relatives waved frantically, searching for passengers off the latest ship to arrive.

Savage moved through the crowd like an eel through a can of grease, avoiding cuffs and curses.

He was small for his age and nippy on his feet; he needed to be to survive alone. His gaze darted everywhere. Professionals worked in pairs, one distracting the mark, the other dipping a hand into a pocket or handbag. They resented Savage because he worked on his own, relying on public entertainers for distraction.

The quayside was always busy with buskers and jugglers and fire-eaters, and sometimes a brass band to welcome the high and mighty.

He chose a family. The mother was harassed and concerned only with counting the number of bags and boxes she tried to carry while calling for a porter. The father held a small daughter by the hand as she tugged him towards clowns somersaulting over each other.

'Look at the funny men, Daddy!'

His whole attention was fixed on keeping his girl safe. Savage eased between smelly bodies, following closely, waiting for the right moment. His hand dipped into a pocket of the father's coat, snatched a wallet and immediately he dropped back into the crowd.

He grabbed the nearest urchin and pushed him so he stumbled. 'Run,' he hissed. 'Run like hell!' The urchin bolted.

Savage shouted, 'Stop thief!' and joined the chase. Off the dock, he gave up as soon as he reached the shelter of an empty doorway. He pocketed the handful of banknotes and chucked the empty wallet in a garbage can. . . .

*

. . . The batwings moved and Helen Dexter stepped into the Bonanza. She paused briefly to look around and her distaste was obvious; at that moment, Savage began to admire her nerve. She'd objected when he told her what he wanted; she'd agreed when he told her why.

She appeared freshly bathed, short hair brushed, finely clothed and as cool as if she were back East, instead of walking into a western saloon where men kept their hats on and swore and used the nearest spittoon or the floor. The noise level fell suddenly as some of the drinkers noticed her and nudged the one next to him. Then she saw Mary-Lou and marched directly towards her.

Mary-Lou was not expecting a confrontation, but recovered quickly, showing her teeth in a smile. She exaggerated her drawl. 'Waal, if it ain't the first Mrs Dexter come a-calling.'

She was jolted back on her heels when Helen slapped her face.

'The *only* Mrs Dexter! If Harry married you, which I doubt, that would constitute bigamy. So you were no more than his whore!'

Mary-Lou flushed. She cursed. If this stuck-up cow wanted a set-to, she'd come to the right address. She swung a roundhouse that would have ended the fight before it started, but Helen dodged.

She was light-weight and quick on her feet. With

54

Mary-Lou off-balance, she gave the bigger woman a shove that sent her crashing into a chair. Men scattered, pushing back tables to form an impromptu ring about the two women, calling, 'Fight, fight!'

Ben Ford lifted his axe-handle, and paused. He didn't feel he could lay out a woman, and had the notion his customers wouldn't want that anyway. He sighed; this was an occasion when he had to accept the damage.

Mary-Lou bounced back. She'd seen enough bar-room brawls to know how to handle herself and intended to demolish this Easterner. Called herself Mrs Dexter, after Harry had walked out! She went in fast, aiming a kick at her opponent's stomach.

Helen stepped back, then rushed in to rake her fingernails down Mary-Lou's cheek, leaving bloody streaks in her paintwork.

'You bitch,' the saloon-woman bawled, and grabbed the top of Helen's dress. The material tore as she tried to get clear, showing what the well-dressed Eastern women wore underneath.

Watching men stamped and cheered the best entertainment since the circus came to Calamity. Even the card players chucked their hands in to watch, and Savage joined them; but his gaze was steady on Johnny Nelson.

The gambler drained his glass and raised his voice, 'I'm taking two to one on Mary-Lou. Call your bets now.'

Helen was dragging the saloon-woman back-wards by her long peroxided hair as if she meant to scalp her, but Mary-Lou twisted around, jabbed with a knee and then got an elbow in Helen's face.

Savage wormed his way between excited onlook-ers, each cheering the woman of his choice and calling bets. He closed in on Nelson's back.

Mary-Lou worked herself close enough to use her teeth, clamping on an ear, and Helen lost her temper and shrieked, 'You damned cow!' She aimed clawed fingers at Mary-Lou's eyes. Her hand fell short and low and ripped away the top of her gown so her opponent's breasts spilled out.

A roar of approval went up and men shouted enthusiastically, 'Tear 'em off, gal!' Savage made his move — he had the distraction he wanted — as soon as Nelson had no thought for anything but the fight.

His fingers moved delicately, using the slightest pressure as he felt for and took a grip of the folded paper in Nelson's pocket.

Smoothly he drew it out, gave it a quick glance to make sure he had what he wanted and wriggled free of the crowd.

Mary-Lou was trying to twist Helen's head right off her neck when the batwings opened. Sheriff Ballinger had arrived to break up the fight and Savage passed him on the way out. . . .

. . . Ballinger could hardly believe his eyes. Two half-naked women brawling, cheered on by a crowd hooting with laughter and calling bets.

He forced his way through, shouting, 'Quit this right now – the fun's over.' If they had been men he would have laid the barrel of his Colt alongside their skulls, but he hesitated to do that with women. He wished he hadn't sent Yancey away.

One of the women was screaming and kicking; the other struggled to break a neck-lock.

Ballinger tried again. 'If you don't quit, I'll throw both of you in jail to cool off.'

They ignored him and Ballinger realized talk wasn't about to achieve anything useful. He took a deep breath and made a grab for the nearest arm – but the combatants swung around, locked together, and his hand cupped a sweaty breast.

Immediately they stopped fighting and glared at him.

One said, 'Keep your paws to yourself,' and the other, 'How like a man to get where he isn't wanted!'

One grabbed his arm and pulled, while the other stuck out a foot for him to trip over. 'We'll teach this one to mind his own business.'

Ballinger stumbled and lost his balance. A hand shoved in the small of his back and he sprawled headlong in the sawdust. He heard laughter and saw Wally Kemp scribbling a note. Mac called gleefully, 'Women one, Sheriff nil!'

Ballinger scowled and spluttered, 'Damn women!' He was struggling upright when Johnny Nelson let out a screech, 'My map – it's gone!'

Mary-Lou regarded him with disgust. 'And you're supposed to be the sharp one?' She exchanged a glance with Helen and they both broke into smiles. They linked arms, adjusting their dresses as they headed for the door.

'Come on, honey, we'll split a bottle at the hotel!'

CHAPTER 6

PALMER'S LITTLE JOKE

Hodge was in a good mood. He slapped his thigh and beamed a broad smile at Savage.

'As neat a trick as any I've seen, kid – the way you conned that sporting gent was a treat. Maybe he won't shout so loud in future.' He blew a smoke ring. 'But you might consider stepping lightly around him for a while.'

Savage shrugged. Johnny Nelson didn't worry him. It was the map that puzzled him; he'd studied it last night in his room, and again this morning. It showed the location of the mine and the main galleries, but its importance eluded him.

He handed it to the expert. 'What can you tell me about this?'

Hodge unfolded the paper and held it up to the light.

'It's not one I've handled,' he said after a while. 'I make a small mark on all those, so I'll know them again. A copy of a copy maybe, but it ignores much of the mine – guess it agrees with what I remember of the Last Hope. What yuh figuring on doing?'

'Figure to ride out and look around there.'

'You're on your own then,' Hodge said firmly. 'I ain't aiming to run into Blackie's gang of murderers.'

Savage didn't mention he had the intention of seeking out one of the gang. 'Assuming I find the place, what'll I need? A lamp, for sure.'

'And matches,' Hodge said, ticking off items on his fingers. 'Helmet, overalls—'

'Forget the fancy stuff.' Savage was impatient to be away. 'I'm not doing any mining.'

'Your choice.' Hodge stubbed out his cigar before filling a lamp with oil. He wrapped loose matches in a sheet of oiled paper. 'Never forget, underground, a damp match can be the death of you.'

Savage folded the map and pushed it into one pocket, the matches into another. He picked up his lamp and was walking to the door when Hodge asked, 'Ain't you forgotten something?'

Savage smiled. 'I'll pay you when I get back,' he said, and strode the length of the plankwalk to the livery. He hired a horse and rode into the morning haze, heading for the Bloody Hills.

The road to Vermilion lay between rugged hills and twisted and turned as it surged uphill. The surface was gravelly and uneven and, where it narrowed was a bend, a favourite place with hold-up men. Blackie didn't want to disappoint the driver of the expected stagecoach.

This stage was carrying wages for the men working the one mine in the area producing ore, and it seemed easier to dispose of coin and paper money.

Big Jake had his feet planted as firmly as a pair of oaks; his muscles bulged with effort as he levered on a crowbar, trying to shift a massive lump of rock. It looked ready to fall, but was reluctant as any mule to make the first move. Jake wiped sweat from his hands and tried again; the rock teetered and then fell back.

'Goddamn it,' Jake said, and Poison Palmer sniggered. He enjoyed it when something went wrong for Blackie's favourite.

Virgil uncoiled his lariat. 'Let me try something,' he drawled.

The ex-cowboy chose a place to stand, below the rock, and cast his noose. It settled easily and he jerked it tight. 'Now, Jake, you push and I'll pull.'

Big Jake spat on his hands and took a fresh grip on the crowbar. He heaved, and the rock moved. Virgil hauled on his rope to stop it falling back. The rock hung poised for a moment, wobbled, and then crashed down as Virgil leapt clear. A cheer went up, except from Palmer.

'Good work,' Blackie said. 'Now we'll move further back. The stage will never get past that, and it's too narrow to turn here.'

He glanced briefly around him. 'The bend will hide the obstruction till the last moment – and you can bet the driver will be going as fast as he can flog his horses. Suddenly, we'll be behind them, cutting off any retreat.'

The robbers walked back along the trail, each man choosing a hiding place among broken rocks on either side.

Blackie stared hard at Palmer. 'And you, no killing. I don't want to have to tell you again.'

'Sure, boss, no killing. Got it.'

'Well, don't forget. Grabbing money doesn't upset people the way murder does.'

Palmer ducked down behind a rock so Blackie couldn't read his face. Typical Easterner, thought he was so smart. Palmer's lip curled and he made a gurgling noise as he suppressed laughter. He'd already decided on his bit of fun. This gang had its uses; a posse might not give up easily on one man where they would be reluctant to press a bunch of outlaws too hard.

He admitted Blackie was a brain when it came to setting a trap, but he relied on others to spring it, like himself, who could scare armed guards just by staring at them. It was a gift he had; and he could so easily slide from scaring into the sort of violence he enjoyed – pretending to be sorry afterwards, of course.

Palmer loathed waiting; when he wanted something, he wanted it *now*.

The sun beat down, roasting him, and making him jerk about irritably. He wanted to shoot somebody, anybody, it didn't matter who. Then he heard the noise of wheels crushing loose rock on the trail, iron-shod hoofs pounding along, and cackled with laughter.

He was tempted to cripple the lead nearside horse as it swept into view. Better not: Blackie wanted the gang behind the coach and, he had to admit, that made a kind of sense.

He had a revolver in his hand when the horses galloped by, the coach swaying and rattling. He saw the driver with one guard up front; another armed guard at the back; maybe more inside.

Palmer jerked up his neckerchief and stood. His eyes glowed with anticipation. He just knew some idiot was going to show fight, and he'd thought of a joke Blackie wouldn't appreciate.

The stage rounded the bend at speed. He heard a shout of dismay, the squeal of horses and a splintering noise.

Blackie stepped from hiding in his silk mask and called, 'Don't resist and you won't be hurt. Step to one side with your hands high.'

There was confusion and dust and, for a long moment, the guards were too shaken to do anything.

One of the horses had been injured, and the coach lay tilted on it side, one wheel spinning and a door jammed against the rock face. Other bandits showed, rifles and revolvers covering the stunned guards.

'Line up against the wall,' Blackie ordered.

A couple of robbers brought up pack horses, and Big Jake unloaded boxes and sacks from the coach. Others began to load their horse with coin and paper money, balancing the weight.

The injured horse made noises of distress and Blackie strolled up to its head, raised his revolver and shot it.

With everyone's attention on the transfer of the loot, Palmer picked his target. One of the guards was young, maybe nineteen, and itching to be a hero; his gaze darted from one masked robber to another, looking for a chance to go for his gun.

Palmer drifted closer. 'There's no point in carrying a gun if you ain't got the nerve to draw.'

The youngster glanced at him and moistened his lips, a rabbit hypnotized by a snake.

Palmer pushed again. 'A guard's paid to protect whatever the stage carries, right? I guess you're taking the money but not the risk.'

The fingers of the young guard clawed the air above the butt of his Colt.

'Ignore him,' the driver warned. 'This one's poison.'

'That's me,' Palmer agreed, eyes staring above his neckerchief. 'And you've got more yellow than a singing canary—'

The youngster went for his gun, but Palmer's was already in his hand. He triggered twice, and the guard dropped his gun and screamed; for a moment it looked like he was dancing and then he hit the ground and curled up, hugging himself and crying.

'Crawl,' Palmer said. 'I want to see you crawl . . . the way you'll be crawling for the rest of your life!' He brayed his creepy laugh.

He'd placed his shots carefully, one in each ankle, smashing the bones beyond repair. 'I guess you won't forget me, son.'

He was pleased with himself, and enjoyed watching the youngster writhe on the ground, sobbing, knowing he'd never walk again.

He turned towards Blackie. 'See, boss, I don't have to kill everyone!'

Blackie seemed to be breathing hard under his mask. He turned away. 'Sometimes, Palmer, I don't think you're quite human.'

Palmer smirked. 'Just my little joke, boss.' He looked around, appealing to other members of the gang, but no one laughed.

Jake said, 'All loaded, boss,' and Blackie swung up on to his horse. 'Let's get out of here.'

One by one, unhurried, the robbers mounted and whipped the pack horses before them. They rode away with their loot, heading back to the hidden valley.

*

Savage's hired horse stopped when it reached the top of the trail. It seemed disappointed after the effort to reach this plateau, and nosed tiredly at some moss below a stunted tree, searching in vain for grass.

Savage dismounted and walked to the edge. In one direction lay the valley, a sheer drop; around him walls of red sandstone rose and fell like the waves of an ocean. There were cracks in the walls, canyons, but which might lead through to the valley was impossible to see.

He walked along the edge and movement below caught his eye; a solitary rider following a line of bones scattered along the base of the wall. After a moment, he realized they were Caesar's bones, picked clean by scavengers and distributed to mask the place where Palmer had stopped him.

Savage studied the rider, young with a fringe of beard: Yancey. So the sheriff had listened and sent his deputy to look for a way into the valley. He didn't appear to be looking hard, but then Savage wasn't sure *he* could now find the way in.

He regarded what was left of Caesar without pity. The horse had served him well, and Poison Palmer would pay when he caught up with him, but he no longer felt any tug of emotion; Caesar belonged to the past.

He turned his back on the rim and took out the copy of Dexter's map. It showed the general area above ground, and some of the underground workings. He found the entrance to the Lost Hope

66

without much difficulty; it was just a hole with rocks, timber and rusting tools scattered around. He peered into darkness and thought it looked no more than a cave.

A brief inspection revealed undisturbed dust, so he left his shotgun with the horse. He wore a Bowie at his belt and that might be useful. Inside, he lit Hodge's lamp; by its light he saw, further back, a tunnel sloping down under the earth and he followed it.

At first there were old rails, then bare rock. The roof lowered and the tunnel narrowed. It went down for some distance before he came to side passages and places where old timbering had collapsed.

He paused to study the map and went on again, wondering about Harold Dexter. What did he think he was doing here? Who had sent him the map, and why?

A wall glittered where it had been salted, and there were places where the main tunnel forked. It was a long time since this mine had been worked.

The air was cool and slightly musty. He reached a cave-in and took a side passage, still descending. His lamp revealed another blockage and he detoured, came to a blank wall.

He retraced his steps to the last junction, and paused, wondering if there was any point to going on, anything at all to discover. His map no longer seemed reliable.

He started to go back and, at the next fork,

found he wasn't sure which pasage to take. He stared around, undecided, and then realized he was lost underground.

CHAPTER 7

THE LAST HOPE

Savage stared at rough blank walls and felt a chill that had nothing to do with low temperature. Beyond the circle of lamplight darkness pressed about him like a shroud.

He grew increasingly aware of a weight of rock above his head, threatening to fall at any moment and crush the life from him. Or worse, pin him down to wait, helpless, for the end. Only Hodge knew where he was, and Hodge wouldn't lift a finger unless he was paid.

He shut down his imagination, got out his map and studied it again. He was still uncertain which way to go, but one thing was sure; if he didn't move he would die down here. He tossed a mental coin and went forward.

After a while he felt sure he hadn't come this way; he discovered more twists and turns, side passages with dead ends, blocked tunnels and the bones of small animals.

He told himself there must be more than one exit and kept going, aware that the oil in his lamp couldn't last for ever. He didn't hurry. One misstep underground could spell the end.

He wriggled around fallen blocks to find a small cave, natural rather than hewn by miners. There were patches of mud where rain had run down to form a pool some time in the past.

He raised his lamp and looked up but could see no opening. That was no problem; he'd got out of tight corners before and he'd survive this one. Hope buoyed him until his lamp began to splutter and the light flicker and then fade to a dim glow. He began to hurry while he still had a faint light to see by.

Then the lamp failed, leaving him in the dark. He paused, trying to think clearly. Feeling his way back might be a safer option, but not likely to get him out. Forward into the unknown held an obvious danger; he wouldn't know until he fell if there was a sudden drop before him. But for the best chance of finding an exit he knew he must explore new ground.

He left the lamp behind and edged forward, one step at a time, left hand touching a wall. It was rough under his fingertips and he reduced pressure; at times the surface crumbled away and he hurried past a small fall.

Fear clawed at his guts when he realized he could be buried under a larger fall, and he had to make an effort to suppress it. Panic could only lead to disaster.

The roof suddenly swooped lower and hit his head; Hodge had been right – he should have borrowed a helmet. Darkness made him impatient. He wanted out, and he had to control himself. At one point he found he was choking, as if bad air had collected in a hollow.

The tunnel narrowed, confining him as if in a coffin and he had to wriggle forward inch by inch until he could stand again. From time to time he paused to strike a match, and the brief light encouraged him when he saw there was still a way forward.

His back and neck ached from shuffling along stooped over where the roof was low. He guessed the cliff was honeycombed and that there must be other ways out, and he imagined meeting Palmer and devising ways of dealing with him.

He touched crevices and felt a breeze from somewhere above, but trying to climb brought only a fall of dust. In time he struck his last match. He saw bare walls and a floor sloping gently away before him. The final dark closed in and time stopped completely.

He shuffled forward, still touching rock, and wondered: how much further? Another step, feeling a jagged crack; another, and the wall curving away from him; another, and the breeze brought a different scent.

Somewhere in the blackness he heard the sound of movement. Someone, or something, was down here with him.

The dining-room of Calamity's sole hotel was almost empty this late in the morning. Just as well, Helen Dexter thought, after last night. She didn't think she could cope with an audience.

Especially as she was annoyed with Savage for deserting her after ensuring her notoriety.

Mary-Lou came through the doorway, yawning, and her face brightened in a smile when she saw Helen; she changed course and headed for her table. Battle wounds had been repaired and, it seemed, a bottle shared might lead to an extended friendship.

'Hi. Shall I join you?'

'Why not?'

'The same,' Mary-Lou told the waiter, pointing to Helen's breakfast. She sat down. 'I figure we'll get quicker service now.'

Helen said politely, 'How's Johnny this morning?'

'Still snoring his head off. He never moves before noon. And Mr Savage?'

'Up and away, I've been told. Early. He has a restlessness that reminds me of my late husband.'

Mary-Lou attacked the loaded plate the waiter

put in front of her. 'Harry? Yes, there is a resem-
blance. I never felt sure when he was going to
move on – that's why I took a copy of his map, and
it's a good thing I did. He believed in that mine,
you know.'

'I know,' Helen said quietly. 'And now he's
dead.'

They regarded each other, dry-eyed, two women
who'd shared the same man, and Helen remembered how it had been in the beginning. . *.* .

. . . taking Harry's hand as they passed between
iron gates and walked up the driveway to the big
house with fluted columns each side of the porch.
She had been proud of him then, but her father
had not been impressed.

She'd disappointed him from birth. He'd
wanted a son to carry on the family business; her
job had been to catch a suitable son-in-law. And
Harry, her father decided, was not the man for the
job.

Or any other it soon turned out. He couldn't
stick any mundane business for long; he began
with enthusiasm, but lost interest quickly.

'Life's passing,' he'd say, laughing, 'and we've
no time to waste!'

Helen's mother lent moral support; she was a
romantic who sighed over true love. Of course,
they were both young when Harry swept her off
her feet in a whirlwind romance. He appeared
adventurous, reckless even, but Helen was sure she

could tame his wildness and make something of him.

It didn't work that way. Harry had a glib tongue and could be convincing for a short while, but his restlessness always proved too much to contain and he moved on to yet another job that didn't last. Eventually, her father gave up and even her mother shook her head in faint regret.

Naturally, everything he did, he did for her. He'd always said he wanted only the best for her and she had no reason to doubt his word. Even at the last, when he'd headed West alone, he promised to send for her 'once he made his fortune'.

So her father had been right and she'd made a mistake, but that didn't mean she could write Harry off, just like that. Someone had shot him and his murderer remained free; that wasn't her idea of justice. . . .

. . . 'Yes,' she repeated, 'Harry's dead, and Mr Savage is looking for whoever shot him.'

Mary-Lou wiped her plate clean with a thick slice of bread. 'If that's how you feel, why not? He was all right to me for our time together – but it's what might be in his mine that interests men now.'

'I don't doubt Mr Savage is looking at this moment.'

Mary-Lou lit a cigarette. 'You and me should stay together,' she decided. 'A woman can't afford to be on her own in this country – that's why I teamed up with Johnny.'

Helen studied the artificial blonde, and smiled. 'I think I'd like that. I never had a woman friend before.' She brooded a moment, then added, 'I wonder who sent Harry that map?'

Savage held his breath, listening. He remained motionless, waiting, but the sound was not repeated. Had he imagined it? It was too easy to imagine things in the dark.

He controlled his breathing, expelling air slowly. He heard movement again and, this time, he was sure he did not imagine it. There was someone, or some animal, down here with him. He touched the haft of his knife for reassurance as he waited.

Then he saw a glimmer from an oil lamp, and relaxed. It was no wild animal then, but some person who knew a way in and so he had only to follow the light to get out.

The light faded as the lamp moved away and Savage trod warily. He didn't hurry to catch up and was careful what he touched; even so, he started a small fall of loose stones.

He stopped dead, but the light continued to move away. No doubt the unknown was used to the earth shifting and starting slides. He followed again, taking extra care, keeping his mouth open to ensure his breathing made the minimum sound.

The man with the lantern seemed to know his way underground, and Savage wondered briefly who he was, and what he was doing, but he wasn't deeply interested.

Whatever his business here, he was a guide leading to fresh air and daylight. Savage kept a distance between them, not prepared to trust his saviour until he'd got a clear look at him.

The tunnel widened and opened out into a cave lit by natural light coming from beyond its opening. He waited till his guide had gone, then crept to the mouth of the cave and peered out. One glance told him exactly where he was.

He had passed through the red sandstone cliffs to come out in the valley where Blackie and his gang had their hideaway.

Larsen still looked angry. The owner of the Vermilion mine had been fuming when he arrived at the sheriff's office, jumping down from a buggy and almost running inside. Squat and tough-looking, he carried a rifle the way a hunter does.

'Wages stolen, a guard crippled, and you sit here talking. Get after that bunch of robbers, you useless apology for a lawman!'

Ballinger settled himself more comfortably in his chair. 'I have yet to be officially notified that any crime has been committed. You wouldn't expect me to start a manhunt on hearsay, I hope?'

Larsen made a rude noise. 'I don't expect you,

or your deputy, to do much but—'

Yancey cut in, 'I just got back from riding the Bloody Hills, Mr Larsen, looking for a way through to the valley. The sheriff had a tip-off, but it still didn't help.'

Larsen swore, and ignored the deputy. 'Listen to me, Ballinger, if you hope to have any chance of re-election, you'd better get off your arse and on to a horse. Form a posse and smash that gang – and string up that bastard, Palmer, to the first tree you find!'

The door was flung open and Wally Kemp bustled in. 'Can I quote you, Mr Larsen?' he asked cheerfully.

'Get out, Kemp,' the sheriff snapped. 'This is official business and I don't want you—'

Larsen out-shouted him. 'Step right up, Wally. Sure you can quote me – I'm putting a price on Palmer's head: five hundred dollars to whoever brings him in to Vermilion, dead or alive!'

Kemp scribbled furiously. 'If he's alive—'

'He won't be for long! And the bank will be making a similar offer for the return of the money.'

Ballinger looked unhappy. 'You'll make this a free-for-all. That's not how the law works.'

'People are getting tired of waiting for the law to start working!'

'Waal,' Yancey drawled, 'seems to me Palmer won't be safe from his own kind when this news gets out.'

Larsen scowled. 'And you make sure it does, Wally. Broadcast it wide as you can.'

'Yes, sir,' Wally Kemp said, beaming, and hurried off to his print shop.

CHAPTER 8

THE MAN WITHOUT A MASK

From where he crouched in the shadow of the cave mouth, Savage looked across a lush valley. Tall grass stirred in a breeze, horses and cattle grazed at peace; high walls of red sandstone protected those inside.

It was difficult to judge the size of the valley because he could see only part of it; the wall curved away from him. Within view was a scattering of wooden huts and a group of men drinking and smoking.

The air felt burning hot, as if the sun's heat couldn't escape from this bowl between the hills. Insects made small whirring noises and the gurgling of a creek reminded him his throat was dry.

Palmer was here somewhere. Savage regretted not bringing his shotgun, but he still had his Bowie. He studied the faces of the men he could see – hard, thin, whiskered – but the one he wanted was not on show. Still, he wasn't leaving till he'd settled with Palmer, not now he was inside the valley, undetected. He'd never get a better chance; finding a way out could wait.

He moved forward, crouching low and heading for the creek. It took only a moment's carelessness for the whole situation to change. He heard the rattle too late to dodge.

The snake uncoiled, reared up and struck once, then glided away.

His leg swelled and pain throbbed like the beat of a drum. He pressed his lips together to turn a startled curse into a barely audible grunt, rolled over in the long grass and reached for his knife.

The fangs had struck just above the top of his leather boot and he slashed his pants leg open to get at already purpling flesh. Two quick cuts showed blood welling, and he bent over to suck out the poison. Suck and spit, suck and spit until his blood ran freely.

He lay back, panting. The pain was reduced, bearable, but he was sweating and his mouth dry, his heart pounding faster. Water! More than anything else he needed to drink, and began to crawl towards the creek.

He would bathe his leg too. But the movement of the grass betrayed him when the breeze dropped and one of the gang, curious, strolled across to take a look.

He looked, and yelled, 'Jake! Stranger in camp!'

Jake didn't hurry, but he was big and sure of himself. He came with lumbering strides and Savage waited, knife in hand. To kill would condemn himself. His leg prevented him running. Fight?

He climbed awkwardly to his feet, one leg dripping blood. Other members of the gang gathered around Jake.

Savage hesitated, and one of Jake's big hands closed about his wrist; the other plucked the Bowie from his grasp and threw it aside.

'You ain't going to need that, fella. Suppose you tell us what you're doing here?'

Even though he believed it hopeless, Savage had to try. 'Just looking for a place the law can't reach me.'

'You've found it,' Jake said, and then his forehead creased. 'But how did you get in?'

Savage decided, get a fight going, put a stop to the questions, and chopped with the side of his hand at Jake's throat. The big man gasped and rocked back on his heels, but failed to go down. Instead he moved forward, wrapped powerful arms around Savage in a hug like that of a bear, and squeezed.

Savage felt the air leave his lungs and thought his ribs would crack. He brought up the knee of his good leg in a sharp motion and Jake grunted, taking his full weight. Savage broke free but his injured leg collapsed under him before he could grapple a hold, and Jake put the boot in.

Savage fell back, half-dazed.

'Little rooster, ain't he?' Jake said admiringly. 'Game to the end!'

Savage rolled aside as another boot came at him, and then he heard a familiar voice.

'It's that goddamned Pinkerton.' Poison Palmer had arrived. 'Let me at him – I'll finish him this time.'

Jake's big voice rumbled, 'No, leave him alone. The boss'll decide.'

Savage scrambled upright, favouring his weak leg; it wouldn't be a good idea to remain on the ground at the mercy of a killer.

Palmer stared at him, smirking, hands twitching. 'I want him to play with.' His voice was dreamy. 'I've got some ideas I want to try on this one.'

The gathering of robbers parted to let one man through. 'What's going on here?'

It was an Eastern voice, a city voice, Savage realized. Jake and Palmer spoke together.

'We've got a good fighter here, chief.'

'We've caught ourselves a Pinkerton!'

Savage knew he was face to face with the leader of the gang without his mask.

Hodge sprawled in his big armchair, eyes closed. He pushed his derby back another notch to show he was listening.

Johnny Nelson wasn't fooled for a moment. The amount of stock crammed into the store indicated

Hodge carried some weight at the bank.

He'd bet there was a gun just below the counter. He figured Hodge had to be interested, but was reluctant to show his hand. He rolled a cigarette and struck a match.

'It won't commit you to anything. We agree to share whatever we learn and act together in future if we both think it worth our effort.'

'Too vague,' Hodge remarked.

'You're a mine expert, and I like to take a chance. We'll make a good team.'

'Team? To do what, exactly?' Hodge's smile reminded Nelson of a drawing he'd once seen of a shark's mouth. 'You ain't figuring to use me to get back at Savage, I hope? He's a dangerous man.'

'I don't carry grudges. He out-smarted me, but he sure went to some trouble to lift my copy. Why? You've seen it?'

'He showed me,' Hodge admitted. 'A copy of a copy. So? The Last Hope is worthless.'

He was still cagey, Nelson thought, reluctant to take the smallest risk.

'Risk is my business, and I've a feeling there's something about this mine we don't know. Something to make a real effort worthwhile.'

'Maybe.'

'And when Savage returns, Mary-Lou will winkle it out of him. Now are you interested?'

Hodge nodded slowly, thoughtfully. 'Secrets about any mine interest me. You might say they're my business.'

Nelson took a last draw on his cigarette, and stubbed it out. 'Then we've got a deal.'

He didn't look like a Western desperado. Neither did he look like a leader who could control a bunch of killers. So there had to be more to him than his appearance.

Not much taller than Savage, slender with a fresh face, pale skin reddened by the sun. He wore almost new Western-style clothing with a revolver at his hip. Savage wondered if he could use it.

In the valley, of course, he didn't need to wear the black silk mask that was his trademark – and, without it, he could pass anywhere as just another Easterner.

Palmer said spitefully, 'This *hombre* is Savage. Let me deal with him, boss.'

'Not yet.' Blackie took his time studying the prisoner, who was rubbing his injured leg. 'Who set Pinkerton's on us?'

'Nobody. As far as I know, Pinkerton's have never heard of you. Guess your fame is purely local.'

Blackie smiled faintly. 'Then why are you here?'

'A would-be miner named Dexter got himself shot. His widow called us in.'

Savage paused. 'So I have to ask, did you shoot Harold Dexter?'

'No.' The answer came quickly, and was definite. Too quickly?

'Or one of your men?'

84

'Not likely – why should they? Prospectors don't worry us – as a breed, they're short-sighted with one-track minds.'

Savage watched his face. Blackie appeared to be telling the truth, but was disturbed by his questions. Why?

Blackie said, 'When I use the word "here", I mean here in this valley.'

'Dexter carried a map of the Last Hope.'

'Who says so? How do you know?'

'Mary-Lou, a woman Dexter picked up on his way west, made a copy. She's in Calamity now.'

Another of the robbers, a redhead, butted in. 'I figure we don't need any Pinkerton snooping around and telling tales. Palmer's right for once – kill the bastard!'

'Maybe later – I want to check out his story first. You Randy, and Jake, search him, then tie him up and watch him.'

Big Jake held him while Randy went through his pockets; he found the map of the mine and handed it to Blackie, who looked at it briefly and put it away.

Savage was hobbled with a short length of rope, walked to a tree and secured to the trunk. He limped to emphasize his injury.

Randy drawled, 'Nothing personal, *hombre*. I just don't like lawmen.'

'I need a drink,' Savage said.

Palmer's voice sounded eager. 'I'll watch him for you, Jake.'

Big Jake grinned. 'Not yet, Palmer – wait till the boss gives the order. You, Randy, get the fella a drink.'

'Why should I?'

' 'Cause the chief might want him to answer more questions.'

The redheaded man obeyed reluctantly, bringing back a pan filled with water. Savage drank and then slid down the tree to squat with his back against the trunk.

He saw Blackie, a telescope under his arm, climb a cliff trail to a vantage point. So that's how it was done – a system of signals – and he wondered about the identity of the spy in Calamity.

Wally Kemp's coffee was going cold. He ignored it, bubbling over with enthusiasm as he pushed a proof of the *Chronicle*'s front page across the counter.

'Just give me a quick reaction, Timber. Have I ever done a better job?'

Timber was used to this and kept his face straight as he read:

DEAD OR ALIVE
Wages Stolen!

The head of Poison Palmer is worth five hundred dollars! Following the raid on the stage carrying miners' wages to Vermilion, and the vicious crippling of a young guard, the mine boss, Niels Larsen, is offering. . . .

86

'What d'you think, Timber? Is this a classic, or is it?'

The grey-haired counterman said solemnly, 'You bet it is, Wally,' and knocked on his wooden leg. 'It's that guard I'm sorry for. Maybe he should get to share in the reward? Or maybe there could be a collection to help him?'

Kemp bounced up and down so energetically the crockery rattled in the Golden Café. Once again his enthusiasm was running wild as he grabbed for a pencil to write in his notebook.

'Great idea, Timber! The *Chronicle* will organize it.'

He calmed down enough to pick up his cup, and swallow.

'Hell, Timber, what's wrong with you? This coffee's cold!'

CHAPTER 9

ACTION THIS NIGHT

Savage made a grimace of pain. He lay back against the trunk of the tree and rubbed at his bad leg. It was a lot better after a rest, but he still wanted to give the impression he could barely hobble along even if he'd been free.

When it came time for an evening meal, Jake left Randy in charge and insisted that Palmer go along with him.

Savage watched Palmer till he was out of sight. The redheaded outlaw didn't worry him. No one had bothered to check his ropes, or the knots; after all, with his leg out of action and no weapon, he couldn't get far. He was still a prisoner in their private valley.

Careless, Savage thought, working slowly and

carefully at loosening another knot. He was in no hurry, content to wait for the heat of day to fade and the cover of night before he made his move.

He could see horses grazing a little way off, and he'd noticed a discarded length of stiff fencing wire beside the tree next to his. He watched the wood huts and the men eating and tried to calculate their number.

His gaze was drawn back to the length of wire and he wondered why. It struck a chord but memory failed him. Somewhere in the past. . . .

He forced himself to relax. It would come. As his eye was again attracted, suddenly, he was a kid in New York.

He remembered sneaking through an open window at the back of a theatre and hiding in the shadows, listening to booming voices and shouts from the audience. There was a smell compounded of greasepaint, liquor and a blocked toilet. It was a gaudy poster that had attracted him, a poster promising all the thrills and excitement of a melodrama.

Now he crouched among the flats staring at the gas-lit scene played out before a noisy audience.

'Spit him!' someone shouted.

The scene seemed unlikely then, the hero and villain duelling over the prostrate body of the heroine; not quite prostrate as she took a sip from a flask and winked at Savage. He withdrew.

But now, he thought, anything was possible. He carefully earmarked the position of the wire so he could go straight to it in the dark. Surprise, he decided, was the mother of invention.

Jake relieved Randy so he could eat; and when the redhead returned, he was scowling and grumbling. 'Why me?'

'Because Blackie says so. Because he reckons a law-hater makes a good guard.'

Jake lumbered away like a friendly bear and, presently, Savage saw a bunch of riders heading out of the valley.

Randy drew his revolver and levelled it. 'Now it's just you and me,' he said sourly, 'and if you even look like you might wag your little finger I'm going to use you for target practice.'

Savage held up his bound hands and declared solemnly, 'I promise not to attack you while I'm tied up.'

The air cooled gradually and stars shone in a cloudless sky. Bored, Randy rolled a cigarette and lit it. Savage wondered idly what the gang were after this time; he catnapped, ears alert.

A change in Randy's breathing woke him. The guard was stretched out, eyes closed.

Savage worked quickly and in silence. He had already loosened most of the knots in the rope holding him. He flexed his muscles and wriggled, straining to make a loop through which he could slide his hands. Randy stirred, and he paused.

His guard resumed his sleep and Savage went to work again. One rope fell away, then another. He massaged his legs to get the blood flowing and crawled towards the length of fencing wire.

It was heavy duty iron wire, almost four feet in length. He placed one end under his boot, and levered, bending it to make a U-shaped handle.

This gave him a firm grip and he held it out straight before him, as he'd seen the fencers do on stage. He raised his arm and struck down; his impromptu weapon swished through the air in a satisfying manner, almost silent, like a rapier striking.

He smiled coldly as he looked from the sleeping Randy to the few horses left in the valley.

Poison Palmer sat upright on his horse, looking straight ahead; his narrow face showed nothing of the excitement seething inside him. He'd thought of a really satisfying way to prolong the Pinkerton's death agonies – and Blackie insisted he ride away from such a tempting pleasure. He felt immense frustration.

'We need your valued service,' the Easterner had said in a honeyed tone. 'It seems likely Mr Shaw will set a guard over his stock – and you have the knack of discouraging armed men from getting too close. Jake, keep Mr Palmer company.'

They were not hurrying. The day's heat relented only slowly and they needed to save their mounts for the return. Beyond the red rock walls of the canyon, away from the desert, rangeland stretched for miles, right up to the boundary fence of the Box S. G.G. Shaw, called 'Gee-gee' by his friends, raised thoroughbreds worth a fortune.

Driving off part of the herd to sell the other side of the Bloody Hills appealed to Blackie. It had looked good to Palmer too when the idea was first discussed, but now he'd lost interest. He wouldn't move openly against the gang leader, but few could match him in cunning.

His mount seemed to go slower and slower and Jake spoke impatiently. 'We're getting behind, Poison. Give your horse a touch of the spur.'

He didn't like being at the rear with Palmer; he wanted to be up front with Blackie.

'You go on, Jake,' Palmer said. 'I'll catch up when this horse gets its second wind.'

He grinned as Jake surged ahead. He followed on for a short while, gradually dropping further back, till he was sure Blackie wouldn't be returning for him.

The robber gang faded into a dusty twilight and soon not even a sound came back. Palmer reined his horse around and applied his spurs, eager to reach the valley again. He licked his lips in antici-pation, imagining the Pinkerton tied and helpless, waiting for him. He felt sure Randy wouldn't inter-fere with his fun.

Savage rejected the idea of taking a horse. He had no intention of quitting the valley until he'd dealt with Poison; and he had no idea of when Blackie's gang would be returning.

He considered Randy. It would be easy enough

to kill the outlaw, but could he make him reveal a way out of the valley? Maybe he should simply hide and create a mystery for his guard when he woke up? Let the redhead explain how his prisoner had got away.

The idea amused him till he heard a tattoo of hoofbeats; someone was coming at a fast lick. One rider. There was no time to deal with Randy before the newcomer arrived, so Savage faded towards the nearest tree and waited in shadow behind the trunk.

The rider came directly to Randy, who sat up abruptly. 'Who's that?'

'Me, Poison. I've come back to have a go at the Pinkerton. What have yuh done with him?'

Randy stared at the discarded ropes where Savage had been. 'Hell, I don't—'

Palmer's temper began to rise. He'd practically killed his horse to get back in a hurry and this idiot . . . Randy saw his face and stepped back.

'You goddamn fool! You've let him get away just when I—'

Savage came from behind his tree and called, 'Over here, Palmer.' By starlight, he seemed to be leaning on a stick to support his bad leg.

Palmer laughed, and drew a knife.

'You want to start running, Savage? I'll give you twenty yards' start and then run yuh down. Now I'll tell you how I'm going to—'

Randy sprang to his feet, drawing his revolver, and Palmer turned on him. 'Stay out of this. He's my meat, mine.'

93

Randy let his revolver drop back in its holster; no one argued with Poison when he was in this mood.

Palmer moved closer towards Savage in a gliding motion and light flashed off the naked steel in his hand.

'I'll tell yuh what kind of blade this is, Mr Pinkerton. It's what a fur trapper uses to skin his catch, and that's what I aim to use on you – only you won't be dead. Not to start with anyway. It's like an experiment, see? I want to find out how much skin I can peel off before you die!'

Savage's lips curled in a chilling smile. 'You're good at talking.'

Palmer rushed forward, eager, swinging his blade, and Savage brought up his wire sword, deflecting it. His left hand balled and slammed into Palmer's stomach, staggering him.

'You'll need to do better than that. Maybe you should stick to talking?'

Palmer licked his lips. 'I'll – I'll—'

He started to drool. He was close to blind rage, not used to his victim fighting back. His eyes glared wildly; now only the Pinkerton existed, and his knife-hand made carving motions.

Savage lowered his length of wire and leaned on it as though his leg still pained him, waiting.

Suddenly Palmer screamed, 'I'm a crazy man,' and charged in to attack. 'I'll flay you alive; I'll carve the meat off your bones; I'll—'

Again the wire sword came up, but this time Palmer swerved around it, slashing furiously.

He was puffing like an engine working up a head of steam, in a fury. Nothing like this had happened to him before; always he'd had a helpless victim to torment.

The Pinkerton wasn't frightened of him and the shock fed his anger. He had a need to dominate, to hurt and, for a moment, his cunning deserted him and left him open to attack.

Savage watched for his chance; he watched Randy from the corner of his eye, keeping Palmer between him and the redhead. So far the outlaw had kept out of the fight.

Savage waited, moving around, dodging wild swings. Then he slashed out, rapier-like, striking Palmer's knife-hand. The skinning blade flew into the long grass and disappeared.

Poison Palmer stood frozen in disbelief, making a low keening sound, a child deprived of a favourite toy. Savage's hand was slippery with sweat; he wiped it down his pants' leg and took a fresh grip on the wire handle.

Palmer stumbled back and Savage lunged, arm fully extended; the point of his sword entered Palmer's left eye and penetrated the brain.

As Palmer went down, clawing at the wire, Savage launched himself at the redhead. No one expected Poison to fail and Randy was slow taking in Palmer's sudden end. He grabbed for his gun.

Savage smashed him to the ground and seized his gun-hand as the revolver came out of its holster. The gun fired once, into the air, before

Savage slammed his hand down on the rock-hard ground. The Colt skittered away, out of reach of both of them.

Randy was taking in air, getting ready to make a fight of it, when Savage punched his Adam's apple. Randy was no Big Jake to throw off the effects of that kind of blow. He dropped back, choking.

Savage reached for a length of rope and tied Randy's hands. He collected the gun and shoved it in his belt. Then he jerked his homemade sword from Palmer's face and kicked the body to make sure his prisoner knew Poison was dead.

When he showed the point of the sword to Randy, he had a feeling the redhead might co-operate. The sky was flushed with first light.

'Time to move,' he said. 'If I collect a couple of horses, will you have a problem showing me a way out of the valley?'

Randy stared at the tip of the wire, and shuddered. 'Not me. . . .'

Shaw's Box S ranch lay snug in a hollow. Blackie sat his horse, looking down on the lay-out, studying the main house, the bunkhouse, sheds and corrals.

It was the corrals that interested him. He ignored the small one by the bunkhouse; that held only working horses for the crew. The two main corrals took up a lot of space, each with its own gate, with a wide lane running between the wire fences. These corrals held Shaw's thoroughbreds. It was a peaceful night scene, the horses quiet and no lamp showing.

Although he couldn't see a guard, it was certain the rancher had posted one somewhere handy, and armed him. These horses represented a lot of money.

Blackie turned in the saddle, searching faces by starlight. 'Where's Palmer?'

Jake looked embarrassed. 'Reckon he's snuck back, chief.'

'Damn the man!'

'Guess we can still use his name to throw a scare into them,' Idaho drawled. He was a specialist in bank robbery, a man with a hooked nose that gave him a villainous appearance. 'They won't know he's not with us.'

Blackie nodded curtly. 'Jake, take charge here. Wait till you see both gates open before you come down.'

He nudged his mount forward and down the slope, with Virgil following. He drifted quietly to the gate of the first corral, and Virgil passed him, heading for the second. One horse lifted its head to watch without curiosity.

The gate fastening was a simple metal loop holding gate and post together, weighted so it couldn't be accidentally dislodged. Blackie lifted the loop and the gate swung back.

He rode in casually, made his way behind the thoroughbreds and began to urge them towards the gateway. Across the lane, Virgil had the second gate open.

He heard hoofbeats as his men came down the slope, and lashed the nearest horse to encourage it to break for freedom. It squealed and bolted.

His breath was coming faster, his pulse beginning to race. This was what drove him, a need for excitement, adventure, the thrill of the chase, the risk and the danger.

A double gunshot sounded, its echoes ringing like a warning bell.

He still couldn't place the guard, but he'd effectively roused the bunkhouse. A light came on, and men tumbled outside, half-dressed, reaching for guns and horses, and cursing.

Someone shouted, 'Poison, silence that guard!'

Blackie thought he recognized Idaho's voice as he adjusted his silk mask and urged his mount forward, quirting the thoroughbreds to greater effort.

Masked men filled the lane between the corral fences, directing the runaways by shooting into the ground behind their hoofs. There seemed to be a mass of running horses and they didn't need more urging. Without saddles, without riders, they scented the open range and raced for it.

From behind came Shaw's passionate cry, 'Don't shoot my horses!'

Blackie was slow to realize they no longer had to drive these animals; the problem was to keep up with them. They leapt away as if they'd heard the starter's pistol. He gave his own mount a touch of the spurs to encourage it to catch up.

From behind, the Box S crew were throwing lead as they gave chase, but shooting deliberately high. When they reached open range, the bunched horses spread out. Blackie, watching like a hawk, was filled with admiration.

Every one of Shaw's horses moved like a champion, smooth-flowing, head stretched forward, ears back and tail horizontal. Blackie promised himself he wouldn't sell them all; he'd keep one for himself.

The gang had managed to get most of the herd running in the direction they wanted, towards the desert and the red rock walls. But not all; some split away from the main bunch and Shaw, cursing vigorously, ordered some of his crew after them. It reduced the number of pursuers.

Blackie glanced round. One of the Box S men was coming up fast, rifle blazing. 'Drop that man, Poison!' he shouted, and the rider eased off.

Starlight revealed even more horses in front of them. 'What the hell?' Blackie pulled up almost to a standstill when it looked as if two herds were colliding.

Virgil shouted, 'Don't stop, boss – this is a wild bunch,' and he triggered lead, shooting into the ground.

A stallion snorted a challenge, herding his mares away from the newcomers. Thoroughbreds swerved. Horses interweaved like dancers. Dust rose from pounding hoofs, blotting out the view.

Blackie went forward slowly as horses mingled

99

and went every which way.

'Our advantage, I think,' Virgil murmured. 'The tracks of the wild bunch will cover ours – it'll take more than a few minutes to decide which way we went.'

As the horses pounded on, sounds of pursuit faded. By the time they'd got the thoroughbreds to the canyon entrance, early light was filling the sky.

CHAPTER 10

BLIND CANYON

Thunder filled the canyon as thoroughbreds and wild horses poured through. Dust coated the red walls.

Following at their heels, neckerchief pulled up to cover his mouth and nostrils, Big Jake promised himself a few minutes with Poison Palmer; that crazy had made him look bad in front of the chief. Palmer didn't scare him; he simply regarded him as a nasty piece of work to be avoided.

The canyon ended and the valley lay before him. The horses spread out and, when they realized they were no longer chased, slowed and began to graze. One by one the gang reined back near the log huts and dismounted.

'Me for some shut-eye,' one yawned.

'I'm starving,' another said.

'I need a drink!'

Blackie stood rigid, looking about and frowning. 'Where's Savage?'

'And Randy?' Jake couldn't see the redhead who'd been left to guard the prisoner. 'If Palmer—'

He took long strides through the grass to where the Pinkerton had been tied to a tree. He saw the ropes, and almost stumbled over a body.

'Jeez, it's Poison! What's been going on here?'

Blackie joined him. 'Dead? And Randy, and the Pinkerton missing. It seems we seriously underestimated Mr Savage.'

Jake nodded reluctantly. Others had tried their hand with Poison and come to a nasty end. This time, someone had bested him.

Blackie knelt beside the body, examining it. 'I don't see how he was killed. Any ideas?'

Other members of the gang drifted up, and it was Virgil who answered.

'See his eye, leaking blood? That's how. I've seen that once before, when a Mex shoved a stiletto in an *hombre*'s eye. That's what killed him, something long and thin.'

'So where's Randy?'

A hurried search failed to find another body. It was a mystery, but few of them worried over Palmer's death – he'd never been popular. One by one the men gave up the search, to sleep, eat, or take a drink. They'd had a hard ride and, later, they'd have to move the horses out to sell.

Only Blackie and Jake were disturbed by the

102

mystery. 'What d'yuh think, chief?' the big man asked.

Blackie rubbed his chin, deliberating. 'I assume they're well away, so there's nothing we can do right now. Later, I'll talk to our man in Calamity. . . .'

. . . Savage was following Randy along a canyon, between walls that zig-zagged, when he heard a rush of hoofs. Instantly he hauled on the rope linking his mount to the outlaw's, getting them both behind fallen slabs of rock. He showed Randy the tip of his wire sword and murmured, 'Don't even think of calling out.'

A bunch of riderless horses swept by between the high sandstone walls in a swirl of dust. Stolen horses, Savage assumed. The herd was followed by mounted riders: Blackie and his crew. They too passed without a pause.

Savage waited for the dust to settle before he prodded Randy into motion. 'Slowly, and quietly.'

Reluctantly the outlaw obeyed. The canyon wound on until they reached a sharp-angled bend; beyond that a narrow opening led out into the desert.

Savage turned in his saddle to look back; the view showed the blank wall of a blind canyon to any casual eye. Only up close would the sharp turn be revealed. He appreciated how the entrance to the valley had remained secret for so long.

'Now move along,' he ordered, kicking his mount forward.

'I kept my word,' Randy said. 'You're clear of the valley. How about letting me go?'

Savage gave him a hard look. 'I seem to recall you agreed with Palmer killing me.'

'That was then, this is now.'

'Right now I represent the law, and I figure Sheriff Ballinger will be pleased to see you.'

'Won't do yuh no good,' Randy said, sulking.

'It won't do me any harm either,' Savage countered, and urged both horses on towards Calamity.

Business was slow at the Bonanza. Ben Ford stood in the doorway, looking out on Main Street and arguing with Mac, one of his regulars.

'No more credit,' Ford said, snapping his suspenders. 'Ballinger says he's fed up with you taking up jail space.'

'Aw, c'mon, Ben, one little drink can't do any harm.'

'I said "no" and I mean—'

Two riders appeared at the end of Main, heading into town.

'Looks like the Pinkerton,' Ford said. 'Wonder who he's bringing in.'

As the riders stopped outside the sheriff's office, Ford saw that the second man had his hands tied. Savage helped him down and walked him inside.

Mac said, 'I'm off to tell Wally – he'll want to know, and he's usually good for a drink.'

Savage pushed Randy forward, past the sheriff's desk, towards the cell at the rear. Yancey, standing, drew his revolver.

Savage paused beside Ballinger. 'A present from the Bloody Hills – one of Blackie's gang.'

The sheriff pulled a sheaf of Wanted notices from a drawer in his desk and compared each picture in turn with the prisoner. After a while, he gave a grunt of satisfaction.

' "Randy" Randall, wanted for robbery and murder. Good work, Savage – lock him away, Frank.'

Yancey opened a cell door and pushed Randall inside. The prisoner held out his hands. 'You might cut these off, Deputy. I've got an itch and can't scratch.'

Yancey grinned, but cut the ropes away before slamming and locking the door.

Ballinger turned to Savage. 'Suppose you tell me—'

Wally Kemp came in with a rush, breathless, notebook in hand.

'Who did you bring in, Mr Savage?' He pulled a pencil from his pocket. 'Give me your story for the *Chronicle* and I'll give you a front-page headline. That won't hurt you with Pinkerton's.' He licked the tip of his pencil. 'Now, right from the beginning. Who—?'

'His name's Randall,' Savage said. 'The sheriff will give you details.'

He pushed past the newspaperman and moved along the plankwalk towards the hotel. He worked for Pinkerton and Helen Dexter, not Ballinger or Kemp.

He climbed the stairs to Helen's room and rapped on the door. She called, 'Come in.'

He opened the door and paused, in surprise, when he saw Mary-Lou was with her. The two women seemed on remarkably good terms considering the last time he'd seen them together they'd been fighting like hellcats. Now, apparently, they were the best of friends; mentally he reserved judgement.

Mary-Lou winked at him. 'Hi, lover, maybe you did us a favour!'

He nodded, and Helen said briskly, 'Your report, please.'

He shut the door behind him. 'I questioned Blackie about your husband's death. He denied any hand in it and I'm inclined to believe him. He also said that, as far as he knew, his men had nothing to do with it either.'

Helen said, 'So who killed him? Will you keep after the murderer?'

'If that's what you want, yes.'

'That's what I want.'

Mary-Lou rolled her eyes. 'You take life too seriously, Helen. What I want to know about is' – she spoke directly to Savage – 'the mine. Did you explore it?'

Savage hesitated, looking at Helen Dexter. Just how friendly were these two? Could Mary-Lou be trusted?

'It's all right,' Mrs Dexter said, smiling. 'We're in this together – women against the West!'

He shrugged a temporary acceptance of this unlikely friendship.

'I explored part of it. I got lost down there so I didn't see all of it, but I found out it leads into the valley Blackie uses as a hideout.'

Mary-Lou looked disappointed. 'The map didn't lead you to a new vein of gold? Or silver?'

'All I saw was where it had been salted – but your map is no longer accurate because of falls.' He paused. 'I discovered someone else down there – it could only be one of the gang.'

'Doing what?'

'I've no idea. At that point, I was interested only in following him to a way out.'

Mary-Lou laughed. 'Waal, if you get an idea, you can tell me in bed!'

Hodge smiled his secret smile, the one that didn't show on his face. The fact that Johnny Nelson was up and about amused him. He lit a cigar and contemplated the sunlit street beyond his shop doorway.

'You're telling me she won't talk?' That, too, amused him. It appeared that Nelson wasn't quite the bigtime sporting man he liked to make out, more a tinhorn gambler.

Nelson hadn't shaved, and looked outraged.

'It seems Mary-Lou's fallen for that damned Pinkerton . . . I ask you! And now she's friendly with the widow – who does she think she is?'

He sounded indignant, and Hodge smiled and enjoyed his cigar.

'So she didn't tell you what, if anything, Savage discovered in the Last Hope? Seems he brought in one of Blackie's gang, so just maybe—'

'Maybe what?'

'Never mind.' Hodge looked past Johnny Nelson, through the open doorway.

Nelson turned and saw Savage, on a hired horse, leaving town. 'Where's he going?'

Hodge could make a guess. The Pinkerton was riding away from the Bloody Hills, in the direction of the mine where he'd found Dexter's body.

But why?

CHAPTER 11

GALLOWS FOR ONE

Savage was impatient to get moving. Calamity's sawbones had pronounced his leg healthy, and a night of lust with Mary-Lou had renewed his interest in life.

He hired a fresh horse from the livery and walked it to Ernie's Emporium, enjoying the keenness of the air before it heated up. He walked inside, past sacks of potatoes and a barrel of cooking oil, groceries and tinned goods.

Ernie had a big nose in a sad face and hovered over his cash box as if expecting every customer to walk off with it. His store carried a range of clothing and Savage tried a new Stetson for size; he also equipped himself with a shotgun and two boxes of shells. He selected a Bowie knife and tried it for balance.

Ernie began to look agitated. 'I hope you can

pay for all this gear?'

'See Mrs Dexter at the hotel,' Savage said, and walked outside. He stowed the shotgun behind the saddle and left town, following the trail he'd previously ridden on Hodge's burro.

As he climbed towards the sun, heat began to build up, trees became scarcer and the grass short and brown. He rested a while beside a stream to let his horse drink before resuming the climb.

Further up, the ground showed patches of bare rock; he saw scarcely any birds. A silence lay across the land and the sky was an immense bowl of washed-out blue.

He reached the old mine and the stone cairn where the body of Harold Dexter had been buried, stood in the shade and briefly removed his hat. After all, the widow was paying him. He studied the hillside with fresh eyes; this time he had an idea of what to look for.

He remembered watching Blackie climb to a high peak in the Bloody Hills, carrying a telescope. Somewhere above Calamity must be a similar vantage point the spy used to read and transmit messages.

He imagined Dexter, intent on hunting out old mines, stumbling across Blackie's spy as he sent a message – and dying without knowing why.

So who was the spy? Savage had no idea as yet; it could be anyone in town.

He walked in a wide circle, spiralling outwards, looking for a likely summit the spy would use. It had to be high; it had to have a direct view of a distant and distinctive sandstone peak.

It didn't take long to find and he stood silent, staring through miles of clear air. So his guess was likely right and Blackie's spy had shot Harold Dexter. Now all he had to do was uncover the identity of the murderer.

Timber took the tray with an empty plate, mug and spoon from Randall. Sheriff Ballinger swung the iron door of the cell shut, locked it and holstered his revolver.

But the red-haired prisoner made no attempt to escape; he seemed relaxed, without a care in the world.

'Not bad service, Sheriff. Maybe I'll recommend your jail to a few mates of mine – I've had worse in some so-called hotels. Timber, I could use the makings next time you call.'

Timber scowled. He fed the prisoner because Ballinger insisted, but he didn't like the idea. As an old soldier, he recognized a killer when he saw one.

'It's a waste of good grub on a hanging job,' he grumbled.

'I agree.'

The man who pushed into the law office was bandy-legged with a face like a horse. Ballinger believed the old saying, 'a man who works with horses grows to look like one', and knew trouble had arrived.

He squeezed into the chair behind his desk as the newcomer bawled, 'G.G. Shaw, Sheriff. I heard you had a horse-thief in jail and came as fast as I could to make sure he swings.'

Ballinger protested, 'He's due a trial, like any other prisoner. The judge decides, so calm down—'

'Calm down!' Shaw's face turned a shade of purple and his hands curled as if tightening around someone's throat. 'Don't tempt me! I've lost a herd of thoroughbreds and—'

'Hanging this man without trial won't bring them back.'

Shaw made a snorting noise. 'Just what are you doing to get them back? Anything? I heard it was a Pinkerton who brought in your prisoner – went in alone and brought him out of the Bloody Hills – not you or your posse.'

Timber stumped away, smiling, and returned to his café as Shaw continued, 'Let's not waste time or the county's money on a horse-thief. I'm willing to be judge, jury and hangman. We'll hang him high and hang him now.'

Ballinger said, 'No.'

The two men glared at each other, Ballinger worried, Shaw in hard-worn clothes that smelled of horses. Then Wally Kemp hurried in.

'Gee-Gee, I just heard you were in town. Can you give me the full story? Have you a quote for the front page of the *Chronicle*?'

He held a notebook in his hand, a pencil poised. The Box S rancher transferred his gaze. 'You bet I can, Wally. That Bloody Hills gang ran off most of my thoroughbreds – and this apology for a lawman is reluctant to hang a horse-thief!'

He paused for breath. 'Here's a quote you can use— If Mr Ballinger doesn't do something to rid us of this gang, he needn't bother to stand for re-election!'

Ballinger began to wish his deputy was present when support came from an unexpected quarter.

'I'll vote for the sheriff any time,' Randy called. 'He runs a better jail than most, and I've no complaints.'

G.G. Shaw exploded. 'You'll vote from Hell then – you'll damn well hang if I have to do it myself single-handed!'

Wally Kemp scribbled furiously, then made a dash for his print shop.

Big Jake watched Blackie descend the cliff, telescope under his arm. He waited in the valley, with Virgil and Idaho and a few other regulars to hear the news from Calamity.

But when Blackie reached the bottom, he didn't move towards them. Instead, he walked to where a long raised mound marked a grave. It was covered by grass and he removed a few withered flowers, replacing them with wild blooms. He took off his hat and stood with head bowed and lips moving, apparently talking to someone invisible.

'Jeez,' muttered one of the gang. 'What's wrong with him? Dead's dead and—'

'Shut your mouth,' Jake growled. 'You know nothing – wait till the chief's finished.'

He had the loyalty of a simple man who sees in terms of black and white, and the chief was white. He could remember a time. . . .

. . . when he left the saloon, counting his winnings. He wasn't expecting trouble: a giant-sized man rarely did. He needed the outhouse in the alley alongside the El Dorado in Wilcox.

He heard a metallic click and looked into the long barrel of a Colt. 'Give it here, big boy,' a voice demanded.

Jake dropped the banknotes and grabbed the barrel of the gun, pushing it away from him as it exploded. He heard a second gunshot and felt a body stumble against his back. He clubbed down the man in front of him with his fist and turned to see a second man falling.

A stranger in a city suit stood at the end of the alley, holstering a gun. He had a pale, sickly face and his eyes seemed to burn with a feverish light.

'That fella was aiming to stick you from behind. I don't enjoy seeing two low-lifes gang up on anyone, especially when one's a back-stabber. Where I come from, we don't stand for that kind of thing.'

Jake guessed he came from some city back East, and looked down and saw the blade.

'Guess I'm a mite slow,' he admitted.

'But big and strong,' the Easterner said, coughing. 'I can use a man like you if you're looking for work. In any case, I suggest we disappear before some official busybody starts looking into the shooting.'

'Ain't nobody likely to bother us,' Jake said, 'but I like the idea of working again. And I owe you.'

'I'm here to look at a bank. You don't have any objection to withdrawing money from a bank?'

'Me? I don't have no money in a bank.'

'That's not necessary. I have a small band of like-minded individuals to help me.'

Jake was impressed: a brainy Easterner running a gang of robbers. He couldn't tackle a bank job on his own. 'I figure if a bank's got money they ought to share it around.'

The gang leader nodded, pleased. 'I knew I could rely on you. Call me Blackie. . . .'

. . . When Blackie left the grave, he moved briskly towards them. 'Randy's in jail at Calamity,' he said, 'and Gee-Gee's urging the sheriff to hang him as a horse-thief.'

'But he wasn't even with us!'

'He'd have been safer if he was.'

Virgil hitched up his gunbelt. 'Then we need to get him out fast.'

Idaho rubbed the side of his nose thoughtfully. 'Seems to me our man in town should be able to do something.'

'Of course he will,' Blackie said quickly. 'When we give him the chance. The sheriff will have the jail guarded, and Gee-Gee's working up a lynch mob. I propose a raid in force. We'll arrive at a gallop and shoot up the town—'

'In daylight?'

'Early, as near to dawn so we can see what we're doing. That'll take attention away from the jail long enough for our friend to get Randy out in the confusion. We'll have a spare horse and he'll come away with us.'

'Sounds good, chief!'

'And without risking our necks because nobody need get hurt. We shoot out windows and make plenty of noise so no one will venture on to the streets. So how many are riding with me?'

'Me.'

'And me!'

Blackie signalled Jake and they strolled aside. 'There's something else, Jake. I've an idea to scare the hell out of those would-be vigilantes. What do you say to. . . .'

When Savage returned to Calamity he heard excited voices and the noise of sawing and hammering. A crowd almost blocked the street. Men clutching bottles or glasses gathered outside the Bonanza, cheering on a man nailing together a structure of woods, two uprights and a crosspiece on a platform. He reined back to observe the scene.

Mac called, 'Carpenter's building a gallows. We aim to swing that horse-thief you brought in.'

A bandy-legged man hurried from the saloon. 'Are you the Pinkerton? I'm G.G. Shaw, and it was my herd Blackie's gang stole.'

'That's likely. I saw horses driven into the valley, but Randall had nothing to do with that.'

'But he's one of Blackie's gang?'

Savage inclined his head. 'No doubt about it.'

'Then he'll hang,' Shaw said furiously, going red in the face.

'What does the sheriff say?'

'That useless damn fool is scared to stick his neck out, but I'm not. I'm going ahead with this – now let me buy you a drink.'

'I'm not a drinking man,' Savage said, and flicked the reins and rode on to the livery.

He handed over his horse to the stableman and walked to the Golden Café. Timber and Wally Kemp were deep in argument.

'He's a bad one,' the counterman declared. 'And one less of that breed is to our advantage.'

'Maybe,' Kemp countered, 'but I see this town working itself up for a lynching – and that means a lot of folk are going to be sorry when it's too late. Randall should be left to the law to deal with.'

'Meanwhile,' Savage put in, 'this customer's starving. A hot meal, Timber – whatever's on today.'

As Timber stumped around his kitchen, getting a meal together, Kemp asked Savage, 'What d'you say? You brought him in.'

Savage shrugged. 'I'm being paid to find whoever

117

shot Dexter. Randall is a matter for your sheriff.'

Timber placed a plate of pork and beans on the table. 'Now, Wally, leave the man to digest in peace.'

Kemp hurried outside and Savage ate hungrily, listening to excited voices, shouts and jeers as the Box S rancher tried to whip up a mob. He heard drunken singing and wild talk.

He sat at ease over a mug of coffee, using a toothpick. He didn't feel concerned over Randall's fate; men outside the law knew what to expect if they were caught.

The evening dark began to close in and Timber lit an oil lamp. The carpenter finished hammering and the gallows threw a sinister shadow across Main Street.

Shaw's voice, now hoarse, faded and most of the crowd dispersed.

'Nothing's likely to happen tonight, I guess,' Timber said, 'but tomorrow you'll see some action.'

'It's possible,' Savage said, and crossed the street to the hotel. He stood a moment in the porch, looking both ways. A light was burning in Hodge's shop and he heard someone run fingers lightly over a piano in the Bonanza.

The door of the law office was shut and Savage imagined Ballinger sitting in the dark, gun gripped in sweaty hands. There were still a few townsmen on the boardwalk and twilight deepened the gloom hanging over Calamity. Savage started to turn away when the hairs on the back of his neck crawled. He dived sideways and headlong and hit the floor. He glimpsed a flare of gunfire and heard the shot, followed by a *thwack* as a lead slug smashed into the door frame above his head.

He rolled over and came to his feet, shotgun ready for action. He heard men scattering but no second shot came. His ears strained to catch the sound of running footsteps, and he started in pursuit.

A voice that sounded like Johnny Nelson's called, 'Who's shooting?'

There were isolated pools of light, but no one crossed them; whoever had fired the shot had already vanished into deep shadow.

Savage took a few paces, staying in shadow himself with shotgun levelled, but it seemed his attacker had gone. He heard approaching footsteps and a figure loomed, revolver in hand. 'Stand where you are – don't move!'

Savage recognized the voice: Ballinger's young deputy, patrolling the saloons and no doubt on edge with a threatened lynching.

He froze, calling, 'Savage here.'

Yancey came closer, peered into his face and asked, 'What happened? Did you see anyone?'

'Someone took a shot at me. I didn't get a look at him, and now he's gone.'

Yancey holstered his gun. 'There's a lot of extra drinking tonight. Maybe you upset someone.'

'Guess so. Do you normally only carry a revolver on patrol?'

'It's all I need. I'm fast.'

Maybe, Savage thought, but you're right-handed. A man who relied on one gun could be at a disadvantage if ever he needed to shoot with his other hand. It was a weakness, but the deputy was still young.

He nodded, and headed back to the hotel, but he didn't believe it was a drunk letting off steam. He believed that Blackie's spy could have spotted him in the hills near Dexter's grave and decided to end his investigation.

The spy remained unknown, but now he posed a personal danger. He went into the hotel, but not upstairs to his room; he walked along the passage and out the back door. Tonight he'd be sleeping somewhere else.

CHAPTER 12

BULLET FOR A LAWMAN

The Golden Café opened early to feed those who'd waited through the night and some who'd crawled out of bed before the sun. A hanging was not an everyday happening in Calamity.

Savage shared a table with Wally Kemp, waiting impatiently for the end of his news story.

'What time are you taking the prisoner his last breakfast?' the editor asked. 'I'll come with you in case he has any final words.'

'I'm not wasting food on a dead man,' Timber grunted. 'Anyway, they'd be unprintable.'

Savage called for a refill and had to wait. Timber had rarely had so much demand for coffee, or bacon.

Savage's hand never strayed far from his shotgun, even though he didn't believe he was in any immediate danger; there were too many townsmen about to recognize the shooter.

He'd followed Mac home in the dark after he'd been chucked out of the Palace, laid him out on the floor and slept in his bed. Mac was probably still snoring.

First light showed a small crowd gathering around the scaffold on Main Street. Savage saw Gee-Gee Shaw, who seemed quietly confident the sheriff would back down. He heard Johnny Nelson offering odds and taking bets.

A thunder of racing hoofs echoed through the dawn and a flurry of gunfire emptied the street as riders swept by the jail. Gallows-watchers dived for cover as windows shattered with a noise like explosive going off.

Savage spilt his coffee and Timber hastily turned out the lamp as breakfasters hit the floorboards. The raiders turned back, still spraying lead.

The attack didn't seem centred on the café so Wally Kemp crawled to the half-open door and peered out. He had a pencil in one hand and a notebook in the other.

'They're surrounding the jail,' he reported. 'Bullets are flying wild. I see masked men on prancing horses shooting at random, or at anything that moves . . . one wears a black silk mask. It's Blackie's gang all right.'

Even flat on his pot-belly, Kemp tried to duck lower.

'And Poison Palmer! Jeez, but he looks terrible . . . as if he's come back from the dead! His face is a ghastly white. His horse doesn't like it . . . the animal's trying to buck him off but he's tied in the saddle, tied to a stake to keep him upright. He's like, cleared the street, I swear I've never seen anything so scary!

'Another seems to be a cowboy. He's whirling a lariat above his head. Now he's dropped the loop over the scaffold . . . he's pulling on it. A big man has joined him and, together, they're straining, pulling. . . .

'The scaffold's tilting, creaking, it's over, it's down, wrecked! A ring of horsemen with rifles are shooting at the sheriff's office, through the window, into the door. It's obvious now, they're here to get Randall out!

'But they're not getting it all their own way. Gee-Gee's screaming and firing back. Others join in. Palmer's hit, he's falling, his horse has thrown him. . . .

'Now it's Gee-Gee's turn, he's down. It looks like one of the gang shot him in the leg. I can see a rider with a spare horse – we can guess who that's for. The horse rears and crashes into Blackie. He's adjusting his mask and, for a moment, I caught a glimpse of his face, raw like a city slicker. . . .'

Kemp wriggled backwards as lead flew past him, then continued: 'The sheriff's in a tight spot. I can see faces at windows opposite, watching the action. This is the most excitement the town's seen in years. The few bullets flying back don't worry this gang. It's almost a one-sided fight. They're storming the jail! They're. . . .'

Inside the law office, Frank Yancey watched Sheriff Ballinger without pity and thought he looked finished, his face grey. Obviously he'd never considered an attack like this when he ran for office.

Yancey was taut as the skin of a drum, hand on the butt of his revolver, eager.

He'd joined his boss late yesterday and stayed overnight. In the cell behind them, Randy Randall stretched out on his bunk, smoking a cigarette. He appeared calm and relaxed as he called, 'Guess I'll be leaving you before breakfast, Sheriff.'

'Maybe,' Ballinger grunted, 'but one or two of your friends won't be. I can shoot as straight as the next man!'

Yancey frowned. It seemed Ballinger didn't intend to surrender his prisoner. Lead slammed into the locked door, and he could hear the movement of horses impatient to be gone.

A ricochet came off the window bars and made him duck. Enough. It was time to end this farce.

He drew his revolver and came up quietly behind Ballinger and shot him in the back. The sheriff made a small gasp as he slumped forward, his face on the desk before sliding to the floor.

Randy jumped to his feet in surprise. 'Why d'yuh do that? I thought you'd just knock him on the head.'

'I don't fancy him behind me afterwards,' Yancey said, using a key to open the cell door. 'He'd know – anyway, I'm fed up with this one-horse town.'

'Blackie ain't going to like it,' Randall warned. 'You were his ace in the hole.'

'So?' Yancey unlocked the street door and motioned Randall forward.

He cracked open the door an inch and called, 'Hey, boss, it's me, Randy.'

The gang swung around, pointing their guns in the opposite direction. Randall ran outside and jumped into the saddle of the spare horse. Then the whole outfit wheeled about, ready to take off.

Yancey darted around to the back of the jail to get his own horse, tethered there in readiness for this moment, and joined the gang as they galloped out of town. A few bullets winged after them and Idaho turned and fired back; no posse formed to follow them.

Blackie moved his horse alongside the deputy. 'What's the idea? You were more use here.'

'I had to shoot Ballinger, and there was no way I could explain that.'

Blackie was annoyed. 'Damn you, this could cause trouble.'

. . . Helen Dexter woke suddenly to the crash of gunfire. It was dark and noisy and she had to think where she was; a hotel room in a mining town out West. Harry was dead and she was alone.

125

A faint light showed beyond the open window. She heard the snorting of horses, and men shouting. Were they all drunk? She was tempted to turn over in bed and go back to sleep when glass shattered.

She sighed; really, this was too much. She identified the outline of a wash-basin on the bedside table, pushed back the sheet and swung her bare feet onto a strip of carpet.

She padded to the window, standing to one side, and looked down on a bunch of riders milling around and firing off rifles and revolvers. They were gathered about the sheriff's office and a few townsmen were shooting back at them. One man, at least, was down on the ground.

The men on horseback wore neckerchiefs pulled up almost to their eyes, except one who wore a black silk mask. Her gaze lingered on him; there was something familiar about his build. Was she dreaming?

A loose slug proved she wasn't as it whined past her head and ploughed into the ceiling. Dust fell on her nightdress.

She concentrated her attention on the man in the silk mask; he was obviously the leader. 'Blackie', Savage had called him.

A horse reared up and collided with him. His mask slipped and, as he readjusted it, she saw his face; only for a moment, but that was enough. She recognized a face out of her past and long familiar to her.

Her heart skipped a beat because what she had just seen was impossible; she had looked into the face of her dead husband.

Then he spoke to the rider who'd jostled him: 'Careful.' One word, but she knew beyond any doubt. She would know that voice anywhere, any time: Harry's voice.

'Blackie' was an alias. The man behind the mask was Harold Dexter, alive and leading a gang of robbers.

After the shock wore off – Helen perched on the edge of the bed, gulping air into her lungs – anger came. He'd promised to send for her and he'd deceived her. Anger blossomed into fury. The colour returned to her face, her pulse quickened and her hands clenched to make fists. Her voice went up, almost to a scream: 'You *bastard*, Harry!'

The moment Blackie's gang left town, Wally Kemp was on his feet and running towards his print shop. His heart was racing and his fingers itched to set type faster than he'd ever set it before.

Savage was in no hurry. After Timber put his café straight, he lingered over a cup of fresh coffee while other customers began, cautiously, to investigate their town.

'Ain't you curious?' Timber asked.

'Curiosity killed a whole sackful of cats. And, besides, Blackie may have left a man with a rifle behind to discourage pursuit.'

Timber nodded, impressed. 'Guess you're right.

127

Anyway, I reckon that Randall killer is loose again.'

'Guess so.' Savage drained his cup and moved easily to the doorway and looked out. 'But I don't see either of your lawmen taking an interest.'

He moved along the boardwalk. Doc was treating Gee-Gee's leg. An excited crowd hovered around the smashed gallows and Mac was waving a revolver in the air and pointing to a body in the dust.

'It's Poison Palmer, see? I got him – I shot him and I claim the reward! Where's Larsen, that's what I want to know. I want my money. I got him and—'

The crowd ignored him. Savage stepped up behind him and took the ancient revolver out of his hand. It was unloaded and rusty.

'I wouldn't advise firing that,' Savage said. 'It might take your hand off.'

He walked to the open door of the law office and peered inside. Ballinger lay on the floor beside his desk. The cell door was open, a key in the lock. There was no sign of Yancey.

He bent over the sheriff and touched him; shot in the back at close range and beyond help. He straightened and went outside, calling loudly, 'Has anyone seen Deputy Yancey?'

Johnny Nelson grinned. 'I saw the idiot going after the raiders.'

More likely joining them, Savage thought; and spoke to the doctor.

'If there are more wounded, attend them first,

128

Doc. Ballinger's past help.'

Ben Ford snapped his suspenders and swore. He had stepped outside to sweep broken glass from the veranda of his saloon.

'He wasn't much, but he represented law and order here. It's time we got a posse together and cleaned out that nest of vermin. Will you lead us, Mr Savage?'

He shook his head. 'I've another job to do.'

'At least tell us where to get into the valley.'

Savage described the place where the canyon came out of the red wall. 'It looks like a blind canyon – all you'll see till you get up close is a blank wall, so it's easy to miss. Blackie will likely have a guard posted.'

He moved off. First, he decided to report to Helen Dexter; she was probably awake and wondering what the hell was going on. He went up the hotel stairs to her room, paused with his hand raised. He heard voices and knocked.

'Come!'

Mary-Lou sat on the bed, clutching a bottle. Helen paced up and down, muttering to herself and pounding one small fist into the palm of her other hand. He'd never seen her so worked up.

Mary-Lou seemed bright and cheerful.

'Give her time! I heard a scream like a banshee in distress and came to see what happened. Helen recognized Blackie!'

Mary-Lou's eyes were laughing. 'Never trust a man – I could have told her that. It was her husband, not decently buried after all!'

'Dexter?'

'Yep, Harold Dexter. Next question, who's in his grave?'

'Does it matter?'

'I guess not – call him the unknown miner. Harry covered his tracks well, and nobody would have suspected a thing if Helen hadn't come West. So what's so important about the Last Chance?'

Mary-Lou took a swallow from her bottle as the door opened and Johnny Nelson looked in.

'There you are, Mary-Lou. I've been thinking—'

'Don't let it go to your head! Now you've told me, shut the door when you leave. I'm partnering Helen these days.'

Nelson looked from one to another, his daze lingering on Savage. 'All right, if that's how you feel. I just hope you don't regret your choice.'

There was a pause after he closed the door. Mary-Lou said, 'The only thing that puzzles me is who sent Harry that map?'

'The only thing?' Helen seemed to have recovered.

'My guess is the gang's loot is hidden there and anyone who can, will collect a fortune. This is the way I see it: I take a share because I provided the map. You get a share because Harry – the crook! – is your loving husband.'

Mary-Lou paused. 'We agree that Mr Savage is another Harry – up and away at the first chance. But there is a difference. Harry's gone outside the law – Mr Savage represents, more or less, the law. So I say we cut him in for a third because he's already explored part of the mine, and we need someone for the physical bit.'

'I agree,' Helen said.

'Anyway, I'd rather trust him than Johnny. Shall we drink to that?'

She took a swig from her bottle and passed it to Helen, who swallowed and grimaced, and passed the bottle to Savage.

He pretended to drink: his target was the man who had been Blackie's spy and tried to kill him. He intended to meet ex-Deputy Yancey again.

CHAPTER 13

AFTER THE MEETING

The Bonanza was crowded. Whiskey and beer flowed and the noise level soared. There were flushed faces and loud voices. Mac lurched from table to table with a never-quite empty glass, accepting refills as if he were dying of thirst.

Larsen had laughed when he tried to claim the reward on Palmer, but bought him a drink anyway; and so it continued. Ballinger had died, but it was Mac who ended up in heaven.

Viewing the crowd, even Wally Kemp was optimistic that something might get done.

Ben Ford pounded on his bar counter with an axe-handle and bellowed, 'Silence! Let's have some respect for the dead. This is a town meeting, not a circus, and we have a serious matter to discuss. One speaker at a time – Mr Larsen first.'

The boss of Vermilion fired his rifle into the ceiling to get quiet. 'It's past time we dealt with Blackie's gang, so let's do it now. If they can ride into town and kill our elected sheriff and we do nothing we might as well quit Calamity. The town will belong to them! They've got money belonging to me and if you help me get it back, I'll share half of it among those who ride against them.'

A cheer went up and Kemp scribbled a note.

Gee-Gee Shaw, one leg flat across two chairs, didn't attempt to rise; he just lifted his voice.

'It was Palmer who deterred a lot of us. Waal, Palmer's dead, and this is the best chance we're likely to get. I want my horses back and I'm prepared to pay a bounty for every outlaw killed. My foreman will represent me—'

'—because it's safer that way,' a voice at the back finished for him.

Mac slurred, 'I'm with yuh, Gee–Gee.'

Kemp's face glowed with excitement. 'If we rid the county of this gang, we'll put Calamity back on the map. The *Chronicle* will give full support – in print – to all those who ride with Niels.'

'Which ain't likely to be many,' Ernie muttered. 'Are you forgetting a canyon entrance is narrow? A few rifles there will wipe yuh out for sure, so I'll keep a listening watch at my Emporium – pleasure to outfit any of yuh, of course.'

'Guess I won't be much use with only one leg,' Timber added, 'but I'll grubstake those who go.'

Gradually the number of volunteers dwindled, and the meeting fell apart with little agreement and nothing decided. A few went to work, others continued drinking.

Kemp's moment of inspiration came from the memory of a newspaper report; he couldn't remember where, or when it happened, but the gist of it stayed with him and that was enough. Later, he referred to it as a flash of genius.

He looked around for Larsen and saw the mine owner scowling and bunching his hands; it appeared someone had lit his fuse and it was a short-burner.

Larsen had set himself the task of getting a town posse into action, and failed. He looked disgusted and ready to take it out on someone.

Kemp edged between drinkers and nudged him. 'Niels, I hope you'll take a drink with me. I've a bottle saved for a special occasion.'

'A meeting after the meeting, is that it?'

'Exactly! I've got an idea—'

Larsen took his arm in a grip like a vice and pushed him outside. 'That's what I need, more than a drink.'

Kemp hurried along the boardwalk to his print shop. 'Wait here.' He darted inside, releasing a smell of ink, and rummaged beneath a stack of paper in a cupboard. He held up a bottle covered in dust.

'I brought this West for just such an occasion,' he said as he started back along the boardwalk.

'Where are we going?' Larsen, following, sounded as if he were having second thoughts.

'Hodge's place.'

The door of the store that had everything for miners was open, and Hodge sat slumped in his chair, derby pulled down almost to his ears.

'What can I do for you, gentlemen?' There was an edge of suspicion to his voice. 'I was just thinking you'd be arming yourselves and riding off to avenge our sheriff about now.'

Larsen snorted. 'Nothing will stir that gutless crew. This is Wally's idea.'

The editor held up his bottle. 'Genuine French wine, saved for this moment. I hope you'll indulge me.'

Hodge stared. 'It makes a change. I had another visit from Savage earlier. He wanted another lamp – and a helmet this time. He's going to do something, if no one else is.'

He reached under the counter and brought out three tin mugs.

Kemp blew dust off his bottle and stripped away metal foil. He struggled with the cork.

'Let me.' Hodge produced a corkscrew to open it and Kemp poured wine into three mugs. 'A toast,' he cried. 'To the end of Blackie's rule.'

'I'll drink to that!' Larsen took a giant swallow, spluttered, and spat out the liquid. 'It's vinegar! If you think that's funny, I don't.'

Hodge tasted warily. 'Past its best, I'm afraid – wine doesn't always travel.'

Kemp took a sip, and his lips pursed at the sourness.

'A shame, but listen to my idea anyway, because that won't go off. I figure the three of us can manage. You, Niels, have useful contacts among miners. Hodge has a storeful of tools. And I have a printing press that can run a big story. . . .'

Frank Yancey was taking his first meal with the gang, squatting on the ground around a camp-fire and eating stew from a tin plate. Some of them studied him with interest: now he was known to be their man in Calamity, the man who'd freed Randy and gunned down the sheriff.

Blackie walked up to him. 'You can have a turn at guard duty. If anyone approaches, deal with him. If a posse shows, fire three shots one after the other, and we'll join you.'

The ex-deputy didn't laugh out loud; he wasn't ready for a showdown. He touched his hat as he replied, 'Sure, boss, whatever you say.'

He lowered his head to hide his smile, but didn't hurry: this was Blackie's way of showing disapproval. He finished his coffee, saddled his horse and rode slowly along the narrow trail to the canyon entrance.

He didn't know the man he relieved; they regarded each other warily, nodded, and the man with grey in his dark beard rode back to the valley. Someone had made a nest among the rocks, shaded by an overhang, with a view of the approach. Yancey settled in.

Time was on his side; he was younger than Blackie. He would explore the valley first and sound out men who might follow him before he made his move.

He was feeling good. This was only the second time he'd killed. The first time he'd been in the hills above Calamity, near the entrance to a disused mine. . . .

. . . on rising ground where he could see the distant red peak from where Blackie made his signals. It was a slow and laborious method, but saved hours of riding, and he was concentrating on a message when a voice took him by surprise.

'What yuh doing, son?'

He almost dropped the telescope. He whirled about to see a lone prospector and a mule laden with equipment. He'd never seen anyone before in this parched and rocky bit of land and it came as a shock. He was young, and he panicked.

He thought only of being exposed to the sheriff. His Colt jumped into his hand and he triggered; he emptied all the chambers before he realized the first bullet had killed the prospector.

The mule bolted. Yancey put his head down and vomited. Afterwards he checked the body; the man had not been armed. He was still shaking violently and it took a while to get himself under control. Then he signalled Blackie, telling him what had happened. . . .

*

With Ballinger it had been very different. He'd waited for the right moment, stayed cool, got behind him and moved up close.

One shot only, and so easy; all it had needed was calm deliberation, simple steps calculated in advance and carried through. He felt fine, never better, pleased with his control and proud of his performance. He considered himself a real gunhawk now and Blackie didn't scare him one bit: the gang boss appeared to be reluctant to kill – a weakness – so Yancey was the better man.

When he'd first got the idea of replacing Ballinger as sheriff he'd been younger; and the longer he waited the more he realized the position of county sheriff was not enough to satisfy his ambition. He had big ideas that kept growing.

His next step would be to replace Blackie, and then make one big coup and retire. He already had a notion about that: one of the railroad barons had a young daughter and Yancey felt sure he'd pay a cool million to get her out of the hands of a gang of killers.

He was smiling as he dreamed of double-crossing his gang, grabbing the loot and vanishing, leaving no trail for anyone to follow. A change of name and he'd reappear elsewhere, a man of wealth and power. /

Savage was deep underground. This time he wore

a helmet and had his lamp turned low to make the oil last longer. He carried his shotgun and his route through the Last Hope was fixed in his head.

He descended as quickly as he could without taking reckless chances, hurrying along the main branch of the network of tunnels and by-passing those he knew to be dead-ends. He had no difficulty remembering his previous trip below.

When he reached the point where his lamp had failed, leaving him in darkness, he slowed his pace but kept taking downward passages. He figured that any way that went lower must lead into the valley eventually.

It was likely that Mary-Lou was right and a cache of loot was hidden in the mine – probably near a valley entrance – and no one would worry if some of it disappeared before he claimed the reward money.

But it was Yancey he was after. An outlaw who killed a lawman and took a shot at him was too dangerous to be allowed to walk free.

He continued down, around twists and turns, stooping where the roof suddenly lowered, collecting bruises and scrapes where the rough walls came closer together and he had to wriggle between them. The helmet helped.

Was that a glimmer of light? He began to move more quickly.

He heard a dragging sound and stopped, holding his breath. He covered his lamp and waited.

Someone hauling something over uneven ground? He wasn't convinced.

He heard a groan. Someone hurt? Again the dragging sound, another groan. Savage moved forward warily.

CHAPTER 14

TAKE-OVER

Yancey's chance came sooner than he expected. When he was relieved and returned to the camp, he saw Blackie heading for an opening in the cliff face. Big Jake was not around, and no one took much notice when he ambled after the boss. It would be enough, he decided, to see where the loot was cached.

Blackie didn't seem aware of him as he followed him through the cave mouth and deeper into the interior of the Last Hope. Beyond the entrance, a tunnel opened into grey gloom; behind him, daylight faded to a glimmer.

In a moment of carelessness, Yancey's boot kicked a loose stone, and Blackie turned, peering back.

'Is that you, Jake?'

Yancey's revolver sprang into his hand. 'Unfortunately for you, I'm not.'

'Frank! What's this about?'

Yancey felt committed now. 'It's about your retirement. I figure you won't need all that loot, so I'll help you out.'

'Is this your idea of gratitude for the start I gave you? Without me—'

Yancey shook this head sadly. 'Sure I'm grateful. Without you, I wouldn't be here now.'

He took careful aim, remembering. . . .

. . . it was chance that made him Blackie's spy. He realized, later, that Goff could have picked any youngster.

He'd been carefree, alone and drinking too fast while taking a hand in a card game with hardened gamblers. Left to himself he could have been in serious trouble.

A horny hand gripped his shoulder and a voice said, 'Outside, boy!'

Yancey was young and resented the 'boy', but his head swam as he tried to shake off the hand. He was jerked from his chair and pushed across the saloon, stumbling on hollow legs. Beyond the batwings, fresh air began to revive him.

'Who are you?' he demanded, staring at a whiskered oldster; no one he'd ever seen before.

'Name's Goff.' A hand pushed him along the boardwalk. 'The boss wants to see yuh.'

He was urged to climb wooden stairs to a room

above a barber's shop, to face a man sitting in the only chair. He wore a black silk mask.

'Will this one do?' Goff asked.

The masked man looked him over, then handed Goff a ten-dollar bill. The oldster left.

'I'm called Blackie. Have you heard of me, or my gang?'

Yancey nodded, beginning to sober up. He wondered what was coming.

'Can you stay off the liquor if I offer you a job?'

'A job?' He felt bewildered.

'The sheriff at Calamity needs a deputy. It will suit me to have a man in place to report what action the law takes. You're new here with no known connection to me – and young enough not to balk at low pay. Ballinger will jump at you.'

Blackie glanced at his gunbelt. 'Can you use that?'

Yancey fumbled what was intended to be a fast draw.

'You see? Liquor is no good for a man who fancies himself a gunfighter. You keep the deputy's salary, and get a share in whatever we take. Later, maybe, when Ballinger decides he's had enough, you could step into his shoes. How does that sound?'

'I'm your man!'

Blackie's lips, below his mask, curved in a smile. 'That's settled then. Have you heard of semaphore signalling?'

'Heard, yes – that's all.'

Blackie gave him some basic instruction and handed him a telescope. . . .

. . 'But that was then, and now I'm ready to take over.'

'You double—'

Yancey's trigger-finger tightened and a bullet ploughed into Blackie's stomach; he doubled over and collapsed on the ground.

'Figure you won't die before you've had time to appreciate the lesson: no man likes to feel grateful to someone who helps him. It's against nature.'

Frank Yancey turned and walked away.

Johnny Nelson held a still-wet copy of the *Chronicle*. The ink came off on his fingers as he stood in the print shop reading the latest news.

Wally Kemp was running off more copies on his hand press. The room was small, hot and smelly and he was squeezed between racks of type and piles of paper.

The rhythmic *thud* of the press might have sent Nelson to sleep if it wasn't for the startling announcement on the front page:

GOLD RUSH DAYS AGAIN?
Another Sutter's Mill?

Rumour is going great guns here in Calamity. Rumour of a gold strike in a local valley used by outlaws as a hideout – this may explain why

144

the news has not reached civilized parts before! Listen to Mr Niels Larsen, owner of the Vermilion mine:

'This is the purest gold I've ever seen,' he told our reporter, almost jumping with excitement.'

Mr Larsen confirms he has held in his own hands a nugget alleged to come from this valley. He also confirms that NO claims have yet been made; because of the presence of these outlaws it is assumed. He intends to form a syndicate with Eastern mine owners to pressure the government into acting against these criminals. With the military, if necessary.

Will he succeed? Will he be too late? Older readers will remember the Black Hills strike – neither Indians on the warpath nor the US army could stop an influx of red-blooded American prospectors determined to claim their golden destiny!

Remember the glorious forty-niners, when San Francisco emptied itself of humanity and nothing could stem the flood of gold-seekers greedy to make their fortunes? And some of them did!

Will we see another such migration? So far the indications are that this strike will make Sutter's Mill look like small change from a dollar bill!

We wait, poised to bring you the very latest on this golden-bright future. Who will start

this new grab for untold wealth?
See our next issue!

Nelson's gaze flicked from this exciting piece of journalism to a boxed advertisement on the same page:

VISIT HODGE!
Calamity's No.1 Dealer
Everything for a Miner
The biggest stock for miles
Overalls, boots, picks, shovels
Etc, Etc!

Nelson lowered the paper and stared suspiciously at the editor. 'Is this the straight goods? Not just a way for Hodge to unload some unwanted stock?'

Kemp kept working his press. 'What's it to you? You'll not get your hands dirty.'

'Who's your source? Savage?'

Kemp reached for more ink so the gambler wouldn't see his smile. 'A journalist never reveals a source.

'Then I'll have to talk to Larsen.'

Nelson crossed the street to the hotel. Already small groups of townsmen were gathering to discuss the news. He spoke to the hotelman.

'Is Mr Larsen in his room?'

'You missed him. He left for Vermilion before the *Chronicle* hit the street.'

Nelson tapped his paper. 'Did he say anything about this?'

The hotelman shrugged. 'He was excited and left town in a hurry. That's all I know.'

Nelson walked on to Hodge's place and found the storekeeper busy arranging a display of his gear outside the shop; he bustled about as if expecting a sudden rush of business.

Nelson watched in silence until Hodge said, 'Can I do something for you?'

'You can tell me what's behind this story in the *Chronicle*.'

Hodge paused in his work long enough to light a cigar. He drew on it. 'Money,' he said abruptly. 'Money is behind everything, or hadn't you noticed? Do you want to buy something? If not, quit wasting my time and move along.'

Johnny Nelson was beginning to feel frustrated, a feeling foreign to him and one he did not enjoy. He was a man who needed to know what was going on.

He returned to the hotel and looked in the dining-room. Mary-Lou and Helen were sitting at a table, taking coffee and talking.

He dragged up another chair and sat down with them, called for coffee and flashed the *Chronicle* headline.

'Have you seen this?'

'We were just discussing it.'

'So what do you know?'

'We know nothing,' Helen said. 'After all, this is only a rumour.'

147

'Rumour? What rumour?' Nelson sipped his coffee. 'I certainly haven't heard anything on the street.'

Mary-Lou laughed. 'There is now! The newspaper will have started one if there wasn't before – and I don't remember asking you to join us.'

'For old times' sake – I'm curious. Did Savage say anything before he left? I mean, who else could it be?'

Helen said promptly, 'He didn't say anything to me.'

'It could be Randall,' Mary-Lou added. 'Or even the deputy. He seems to have been in with the gang. Why are you concerned? If miners do find gold, you'll take it off them at cards anyway.'

'Kemp and Hodge are being cagey, and Larsen's left town. It seems odd to me.'

'So why don't you ride out there and see for yourself?'

'Maybe I will.'

Johnny Nelson got up abruptly, leaving his coffee unfinished. Outside, there seemed to be more men on the street than usual, some of them strangers. And some were buying long-handled shovels at Hodge's store.

Savage turned out his lamp and placed it carefully on the ground. He removed his helmet, brought up his shotgun and edged silently towards the faint glimmer of daylight.

The dragging sound came again, and another

groan. He was almost convinced there was no danger, that he had only an injured man ahead of him, but still he didn't relax. He hadn't survived this long by being careless.

The sounds stopped. He heard a sob, then a whisper. 'For God's sake – is anyone there?'

The voice faded to a whimper and Savage stepped forward; he peered into a face contorted by pain, but still recognizable. Blackie. He remembered Helen's claim.

'Are you Harold Dexter?'

The question brought a tortured smile to Blackie's lips. 'Not for much longer – Yancey gut-shot me.'

Savage saw the fingers of both hands were locked across his stomach, blood leaking between them.

'Yancey?'

'Double-crossed . . . will you bury me in the valley, next to my brother?'

Brother? Savage began to understand. 'I'll do that. Do you want to tell me how this happened? Your wife's in Calamity.'

'I know. . . .' Harold Dexter winced before he continued, 'Charles, my brother . . . he was a lunger and came west for his health. He knew he didn't have long and formed a gang to get rich quick. He took reckless chances and hid his share of the loot in one of the old mine shafts. Near the end, he sent me a map, and his mask to prove who I was. . . .

149

'But I wanted adventure. I thought, why just take the loot when I could wear his mask and carry on where he left off?'

His breathing became erratic.

'Jake helped. Big Jake has always been loyal – but the adventure was getting out of hand. More and more hard men, killers, swarmed into the valley. Then Palmer . . . someone I couldn't control. There was too much killing. . . .'

His voice faded again and Savage asked, 'Who's that in your grave?'

'No name I know of. Yancey shot someone who stumbled on him by accident. When he told me, I took the chance to disappear – changed the clothes, added a few personal papers . . . nobody would guess who Blackie was . . . I could take my share of the spoils and go back to Helen. I left it too late and it's all gone wrong. . . .'

Tears filled his eyes as another wave of pain struck. 'My brother, Helen . . .'

'Relax, if you can.' Savage could see he hadn't long to go. 'I'll take care of things.'

Harold Dexter's body convulsed, then fell back and was still.

Savage checked for a heartbeat: none. He searched the dead man's pockets, pulled out a black silk mask and held it up to his own face.

In a niche in the rock wall he found bags heavy with coin, and a bulging suitcase; he opened this to release an overflow of banknotes.

He untied one of the bags and shoved a handful

of gold coins in his pocket.

Moving quietly to the cave mouth, he looked out at the valley. Yancey, his back to him, was talking to some of the gang. He recognized Randall.

Savage smiled, remembering the job Pinkerton's had given him: to find the killer of Helen Dexter's husband. His manhunt was over.

CHAPTER 15

INVASION

Savage slipped the silk mask over his face, adjusting it so he could see clearly through the eye-holes, and made sure it was secure.

He touched the haft of his Bowie, checked the loads in both barrels of his shotgun, and stepped into the open. The sun warmed him as he walked steadily towards the small group of robbers.

Idaho noticed him first and drawled, 'What are you meaning, Frank? Here comes Blackie now – and he looks like trouble.'

Yancey frowned. 'Don't talk nonsense—' He half-turned to glance behind him and saw a man wearing Blackie's mask, and froze.

Savage kept walking.

Randall brought up his gun. 'That's not the boss!'

Big Jake acted without hesitation. He slammed a massive fist down on Randall's gunhand and the revolver discharged into the ground. 'Don't be stupid – of course it's the chief!'

The few seconds' advantage allowed Savage to close the gap, and he raised his shotgun and called, 'I want you, Yancey.'

He heard three faint gunshots close together. The others heard too.

As heads turned towards the canyon, Savage thrust his free hand into his pocket and tossed gold coins on the ground as a further distraction. More members of the gang gathered to answer the warning signal.

He watched Yancey's hand, waiting for his draw.

The ground trembled. A low roar of continuous sound swelled and echoed. From the mouth of the canyon poured a mob that opened out to swarm across the valley.

Johnny Nelson didn't push his horse. Miners in a hurry passed him without speaking, their faces set and their gaze fixed on the towering sandstone cliffs. How did they know where to go? he wondered. Could they actually smell gold?

He took another sip from one of his water bottles; he was too sharp to carry only one when crossing desert country. Ahead he saw a horse and buggy, apparently in no more of a hurry than he was. When he caught up, he recognized the driver: Larsen.

He gestured at another bunch of men passing them, and called, 'Is this strike genuine?'

'Wait and see, and don't get in their way – I

know from experience,' the Vermilion boss said, 'getting between a fanatic and a strike is dangerous. Me, I'm reckoning on claiming my stolen wages, and maybe evening things up for a crippled stage guard.'

Slowly they approached the red cliff face; rifle fire echoed, and they paused.

Miners surrounded the entrance to the canyon. They were tall and short, some in suits and others in overalls; they all carried tools. One thing they had in common was a fixed and intense stare, as if they were men who had seen the future and it was golden.

One man lay still on the ground; others shot back at the gang's sentry. They muttered among themselves, restless, beginning to get annoyed because their way was barred.

'I hope you've got a gun,' Larsen murmured.

Nelson moved his wrist, and a derringer appeared in his hand.

He waited for the action to start, feeling tense as miners closed about the entrance. They did not look like men who would be denied their chance of a claim by a lone gunman.

Nelson had never seen a gold rush at close-quarters and was caught up in the excitement. More miners were arriving, swelling the crowd, pushing the early lot forward. His blood stirred, his muscles tightened, his breath was coming quicker.

Suddenly the mob of miners surged forward, storming the narrow opening. A rifle *cracked* once and then the sentry was swept away on a tide of horses and bodies. . . .

'Jeez,' Virgil murmured, staring at the mob pouring into the valley. 'What's this?'

He saw men on foot, on mule and burro, on horseback, even horse and buggy. There seemed to be hundreds of them, all carrying picks or shovels, some with guns, and they appeared to be worked up to a fever of excitement. For a moment he thought it was a kind of race.

Yancey was scarcely aware of the invasion; all his attention was focused on the man wearing Blackie's mask. His initial panic had ended when he recognized the voice of the Pinkerton agent. The sweat on his stubble dried and he made his move.

His right hand flashed to the holster on his hip, confident, and came up with revolver levelled and trigger-finger tightening.

But Savage already had his shotgun aimed and pulled one trigger.

Yancey shrieked as the Colt fell from shattered fingers. He looked with horror at the red ruin of his hand, at pulped flesh and bared bone. He almost fainted with shock.

'My gun hand!'

He was ignored by the gang. They were running for their horses as a stampede of crazy men threatened to overwhelm them.

One or two fired into the onrushing mob without making much impression. The avalanche swept on. Idaho, kicked by a passing mule, disappeared beneath flailing hoofs.

Savage nudged Big Jake, who seemed stunned and slow to react. 'Better get moving – nothing's going to stop this lot.'

He stripped off his mask and discarded it as he headed towards a red rock wall.

Behind him, a few desperate outlaws tried to stand against the tidal wave of greed and avarice. A miner swung a long-handled shovel that removed part of Randy's head. Another lit a stick of dynamite and threw it ahead of him to clear a path; the explosion blew away the last thread of the gang's nerve. Over-run by superior numbers, they bolted.

Savage glanced back and saw Virgil, crouched low in the saddle and riding for his life. He reached the bottom of the cliff trail he had seen Blackie climb and started up; somewhere at the top was the entrance to the Last Hope, where he'd left his horse.

Larsen saw Yancey hugging his bleeding hand and remembered Ballinger; he turned his horse to aim directly at him, knocking him to the ground. The buggy jolted as a wheel passed over the ex-deputy.

Climbing the wall, Savage glimpsed Nelson coming up behind the mine boss.

Nelson saw Yancey stagger upright and thought of all the times a lawman had demanded a cut of his winnings, as if he were as crooked as they were.

He didn't think about it; a hide-out gun jumped

into his hand and barked once.

Savage, pausing in his climb, watched Yancey go down a final time, a third eye in his forehead and considered how to simplify his report: he guessed 'died while resisting arrest' should do.

The view below amazed him: hundreds of gold-hungry men rampaged over the valley, each intent on staking a claim and each driven by lust for a yellow metal, indiscriminately killing anybody in their way, whether outlaw or another of their own kind. Someone had pulled a neat hoax, Savage suspected.

He continued his climb to the top of the Bloody Hills. Maybe Helen and Mary-Lou truly believed he resembled Harold Dexter, but he differed in at least one important way: he had a knack of surviving.